Christmas in the City

Emily C. Childs

Contents

Chapter One

Jeri

There are signs to watch for to let you know you've become a Christmas hero.

When another human walks into a perfectly scented room of vanilla, cinnamon, and a hint of clove, they breathe through the nose. The eyes roll back in the head—one of the key signs. More important than words.

The final one—the sigh and coinciding grin.

When those come, I know I've basically entered sainthood in this old inn's kitchen.

"Jeri, it smells amazing," Sloan says.

She tucks a lock of her pale hair behind her ear, and goes through the hero checklist in about point two seconds.

With a long stride, Sloan crosses to the island countertop in the cozy kitchen. It's been remodeled recently, but since the Holly Berry Inn is over one hundred years old, Sloan kept a vintage feel while updating the appliances at the same time.

I don't know how she does it. But the woman is a master at marketing and ambiance.

"What time did you get here?" she asks.

"About five," I say, grinning. It never gets old, someone reveling in the scents and tastes that come from my hands.

Sloan holds a hand over her slender middle, a bit of the pallid greenness in her cheeks fades the longer she snorts up the steam from the sweet rolls on the cooling rack. I'll swear to my dying breath there is a glisten of tears in her eyes.

"I don't feel sick," she says, voice rough. "If I can just bottle this smell up, I think I'll survive this."

I give her shoulders a squeeze. "You'll survive, but I know for sure this little nugget—"

"Shhh," Sloan says, glancing over her shoulder. "I'm telling Ro and Abs on Christmas."

"Right. Sorry." Since I'm up in the wee hours of the morning, it's been nearly impossible for Sloan to hide the visits with the toilet and her queasiness from me. I've known for a few weeks about the pregnancy, and if she doesn't tell her husband soon, I'm going to be the big mouth who lets the Christmas surprise slip. I lower my voice to a whisper. "I was going to say, you know this is Rowan's kid since he-she is already causing so much trouble."

Sloan sniff-laughs. A new thing with my sassy, take-names friend. A few months ago, Sloan was not the woman who crumbled over breakfast food, but lately she's either crying, eating, or laughing at anything. Maybe Rowan suspects something is up, because the mountain man lives to make this woman smile, and he's been running wild trying to figure out the heightened emotions with his wife.

She goes in for another deep inhale, snorting and groaning on her way up. "Mmmm. What is that? These are not typical sweet rolls."

No. No they aren't. I might be a small-town chef, but I am one of those culinary people who views food as a solid artform. It's expressive, creative, and an escape.

"I added a bit of cardamon and clove. Just a hint of nutmeg in the icing, too. I'm impressed, Sloanie. Not everyone catches the changes."

"I have the nose of a blood hound lately. It's a curse more than anything." She rests her cheek on the edge of the countertop, ogling the fresh rolls from the side. "I think I'm in love with you."

Her lip quivers, and yes, those are tears in her eyes.

I nudge her shoulder. "Girl, no worries. I'll come bake these bad boys every morning until munchkin comes."

"No. No, you don't need to do all this. We have the casseroles, and some freezer things. Plus, Angel is really getting a feel for the kitchen. Jer, you've got your own café now, and—"

"I know," I interrupt, "but I still want to help out here until Angel feels totally comfortable. Besides, it's Christmastime. Busy season. You could use the help."

"It is busy." She lets out a weary sigh, but a smile curls over her lips when she turns to a wooden pallet in the corner. "Bright side—I might be able to use my sign soon!"

I glance at the chic chalkboard face that reads, *Sorry, no room at the inn.*

One of those things that made Sloan laugh way too hard.

Holly Berry Inn has exploded since Sloan came back into Rowan's life. Childhood friends, reunited into lovers. Three Christmases ago, I basically had a front row seat to their delightful love story, and it's been a blast ever since. Sloan has worked with massive resorts, setting up staff, opening them, handling the marketing. And since she's been with us in Silver Creek, she's made Holly Berry a true mountain escape without ripping away the rural feel.

Rowan even hired staff.

He *never* planned for staff. For a while there I thought the man would turn into the town hermit and stop talking all together. But no, now on the grounds of Holly Berry there are new faces to keep up with maintenance, the stables, clean rooms, check-in guests. Enough I was able to turn over the head chef position to an amazing baker, and open my own café almost two years ago. A longtime dream of mine, and I can hardly believe it's realized.

Still, it's hard to ditch Holly Berry completely. I'm sentimental, that's all.

I reach for my messenger bag and beanie, taking a minute to enjoy the look of pure satisfaction on Sloan's face.

"I'm going to head out," I say. "If Angel gets swamped, let me know—"

"We won't."

"Rude."

She grins. "Because Honey's is swamped as much as we are. Go. You've saved my morning. You're my hero. I love you and need you."

"It should be awkward hearing my wife declare love to you," comes a deep, soothing timbre. "But it's just the norm now."

I laugh as Rowan comes in the back door, shoulders dusted in a layer of fresh powder, carrying a stack of chopped wood. The guy is a mountain man. Bushy black beard, but still trim and tidy. He's broad, strong, and lives for flannel. But this man turns into a puddle of mushy slush for his wife and their adopted daughter, Abigail.

Sloan hurries to the door, and I'm pretty sure she sniffs him to make sure her stomach can handle it, then kisses him.

"You'll always be my top lover, but Jeri—she's a close, *close* second."

I roll my eyes, and secure my knit hat over my caramel chocolate hair. It's how my Nana always described it. Dark and smooth with a touch of gold. Everything was food with Nana, though. People shouldn't wonder how I got into culinary arts.

"Later, you two. Keep the PDA to a minimum. You have an eleven-year-old girl who is starting to notice the boys on the playground. She's going to get ideas."

Rowan's jaw tightens. "Take it back, Jericho. Abs doesn't even know what a boy *is*."

I laugh with Sloan. Papa bear is my favorite thing to poke. And I do. Often. "Whatever you say, bud. See you later."

Sloan perks up. "Oh! Let me know how the new flavor goes."

I stop, a little stunned for a moment. My family has sort of drifted since Nana died two winters ago. I have cousins who are a lot like sisters; they'll come visit or I'll visit them, but my mom moved to Virginia. We haven't spent much time together since.

But this, *this* is like the family I had growing up.

To know Sloan remembered I'm starting a new Christmas flavor today for the coffee and hot chocolate bar means something.

"For sure," is all I say. Any more and I might start lip quivering like the pregnant lady.

The Grahams, Holly Berry Inn, the town of Silver Creek—they're my family. Other than my food creations, they're all I really need.

Silver Creek is a place right off a Christmas postcard. Nestled in the mountains of Northern Colorado, it's been my home for the last four years and I have no plans to leave. Small, rural, cozy. A place where neighbors wave even if they don't recognize you. Where everyone knows everything about everyone, and scandal is discussed over café tables or hairdresser seats.

Not without its quirks, but during the holidays it's magical.

Sidewalk shops are trimmed in real evergreen wreaths; their windows are painted in festive scenes. Each lamppost is wrapped in white fairy lights, so when the sun sets this town becomes part of another world. Red, heavy bows are tied all along the iron park fence, and along the edges are little, snow-flecked decorative houses with Christmas scenes in the windows. Elves, turkey dinners, and Santa sneaking down the chimney.

Against the fence a few parents pause to chat over thermoses of cocoa and coffee while their little kids bounce on toes to pick their favorite scene.

With every gust of wind comes hints of pine, spice, and smoke. I breathe a little deeper. The fresh snow on the walks is blinding, but I hate covering any of the morning with sunglasses.

I love this time of year. Busy as it is, I live for this town and this season.

Call it a bit of a holiday stupor for my lack of attention. If I'd been tuned in to my surroundings I might not have taken the sidewalk that wraps around the back of my café. If I hadn't walked around the back of my café, I might've avoided the rogue ice ball.

Then again, if I avoided the ice ball, what came after might never have happened.

One minute I'm absorbing all the spicy, sparkly goodness of Silver Creek, and the next the left side of my face is on fire. Full on burning flames. It's the only way to explain it. Black spots dot the corners of my eyes. From my temple to the hinge of my jaw prickles in sharp, white-hot pain.

I stumble. A voice, one that cracks as if it can't decide if it wants to be high or low, wails my name.

I'm not interested in the voice; I'm trying to stay upright. A lamppost is there to brace against. Without question I'm sliding like a fool, grappling for the iron. It feels as if my brain is throbbing against my skull, and my feet refuse to steady beneath me.

The door of the Honey Pot is five feet away, but it's not close enough. The moment I realize my heel has hit the stupid glob of black ice is the moment when time slows to a crawl.

I'm aware my feet are no longer on the ground. My eyes are locked on the bright blue winter sky; it's almost comforting. Even if my brain knows I'm about to land smack on my back on the frosty sidewalk.

My stomach drops to my knees. Then, I hit.

Funny, but it doesn't hurt nearly as much as I thought. Don't get me wrong, my hips are screaming, but my head didn't smack. My skull isn't smashed in pieces across the pavement, and truth be told, I don't even think I hit my head.

No concussion for Christmas? I'd say this is a win.

Still, I'm frozen in place. A snowdrift swallows my legs to my thighs, my rear is soaked on the walk, but why are my shoulders and head propped like I'm sitting up in bed?

"Whoa, are you okay?"

A few flurries of snow sprinkle across my cheeks, and I blink against the glare of the sun into an unfamiliar—albeit gorgeous—face. The baseball hat pulled over his brow shadows the color of his eyes, but if they are anything like the lower lines and sharp edges, no doubt they're the sort of eyes that break into the soul.

Maybe I do have a concussion, because I think my brain is telling me to fall in love.

Chapter Two

Jeri

I am not romantic.

Not in real life, at least. Do I love observing the love of others? Sure. But for me, I don't need the messy details and distractions of giving bits and pieces of the heart to someone else. Odds are they're going to throw them out anyway. Might as well live wild and free and be a lover of love in general.

The brief heart stutter is nothing more than a zing of attraction.

I'm a woman with eyes, and this handsome stranger popped out of nowhere with a face worthy of fantasizing about. Now that my head is on straight, I know it's not insta-love I'm feeling, it's attraction and relief.

So, all those weird little flurries in my stomach need to calm the heck down.

"Hey, you okay?" he tries again.

Here I am ogling his delightful face, keeping quiet, and he's probably thinking I've scrambled my brain.

"Yeah." I start to sit up. Handsome Face keeps his hand on the space between my shoulders. Even without gloves warming his skin, his hand prickles heat up and down my spine. "I'm good. Thanks for the catch."

"Holy crazy cow! Miss Jeri!" A kid skids across the frosty sidewalk. Packed in snow clothes, his freckled face redder than his carrot top head. Not a second later—as expected—three more kids slide to my rescue.

"Lucas," I say through a groan as Handsome helps me stagger to my feet. "I should've known."

"We, we . . ." Lucas Grey leans over his knees, trying to catch his breath. "We totally didn't see you, Miss Jeri."

"It was Tyler freaking Long!" says a smaller boy, wrapped up like a mummy in scarves and padded clothes.

"Tristan," I say, rolling my eyes. "I've told you boys not to let them get to you."

As we speak, three older boys beeline it in the opposite direction. Imagine the Christmas Story—Lucas is Ralphie and crew. Tyler is the bully Farkus. They attack every year with apocalyptic snowball wars.

Should've been watching. A mistake I will not be repeating.

"Tyler!" I shout. "I'm talking to your dad when he comes in at noon!"

The tallest of the runaways, older than Lucas and his gang by two years, stares at me with wide eyes. "Please Miss Jeri! I'll take out the dumpsters every night for a week."

Okay, he's nicer than Scut Farkus, but still. I simply point a stern finger, mouth tight, at the kid until he and his posse disappear into the pine trees surrounding the edge of town. When I turn around the three smaller boys are staring at the sidewalk, kicking at bits of snowball.

"She could've been hurt," my handsome stranger is saying. "You've got to watch what's around you."

"We're sorry," Lucas says in a bit of a whine. "But you don't get it, Mister. Long said, he said he was going to bury us! What kind of men would we be if we didn't retaliate?"

I bite the inside of my cheek, trying not to laugh. The way the guy moves his tongue around behind his lips, I guess he's fighting one of his own. "Don't be the kind of men that hit the ladies in the head with ice balls."

"M'kay," Lucas and his friends grumble at the same time.

"All right, you beasts. Get out of here." I wave the kids away. "You're going to be late for school. Go. Get. Or I'm talking with your folks too."

The boys sprint away, skidding and sliding over the ice as they scramble for their backpacks alongside a berm of dirty snow from the plow. Once they're out of sight, my attention is promptly returned to the sting of my face. Only because strong, warm fingertips are touching the epicenter of pain.

The guy winces. "This is going to be an epic battle wound in the morning. We need to get some ice on it."

"I've had enough ice for one morning, thank you very much."

He smiles, and oh, *oh*, I never knew smiles packed such a punch. Big, bright, and white, with the perfect touch of reservation. Like he has a secret and loves to make people wonder about it.

Smiles, fingertips—this guy is doing weird things to me, and I don't even know his name. I clear my throat and take a cautious step to the side.

"Uh, thanks for the catch. I really don't have time for a brain injury right now," I say lightly, but make it ten times more awkward when I fumble on the ice again.

He jolts his hands out, then chuckles nervously when I secure my balance. "Let me make sure you get some ice for your face, or I'll sit and worry."

"A worrier, huh?"

"Big time. Annoying, needy. It's all me."

He's joking, I think, and when he laughs, I do too. "Or maybe you have a hero complex."

"I do love a good hero. Being one is even better." With his chin he points to the Honey Pot. "I bet they can hook you up with an ice pack."

"I bet they can," I say. "I'm close to the owner."

He nods as if agreeing this is the best course of action, until I whip out the key and jingle it in the old lock.

"Ah. Seems like you're really close to the owner."

I grin, and open the door. "Come on. The least I can do is get you a cappuccino. Heroes get drinks on the house today."

"I'm not one to say no to a cappuccino, but really I'm coming to make sure you don't fall again. You know, hero stuff."

I roll my eyes. "I'm no damsel, trust me."

"No. The way you scared off a bunch of teenagers, I wouldn't say you're a damsel."

He laughs and tilts his hat up a bit, so I glimpse the upper half of his face.

I was right. Sometimes I hate it when I am. Those eyes are brownish gold like caramelized sugar, and they do break right through my chest. *Out of bounds in a big way, Jericho.* There isn't time, and there isn't a point in entertaining thoughts about his eyes, lips, his hands. Ugh, those hands are really strong, and I bet they can do—*oh my, stop!*

If history is any indicator of the future, romance and I are like oil and water.

Why am I thinking romance anyway? I don't even *know* this guy.

As if he reads my mind, he holds out his hand. "I'm Chase, by the way. Chase Thorn."

I take his hand, ignoring the flutter in my chest. "Jericho Hunt. You can call me Jeri."

A little twist in the corner of his mouth reveals a dimple. Well, of course he has a dimple. He wasn't quite perfect enough.

Chase Thorn. Stranger, rescuer, mystery. What is he doing here? I know everyone in town. Odds are he's passing through, but why?

I don't like how the thought that he's temporary squeezes my chest in disappointment.

No mistake, there's something wrong with me.

After years of keeping my heart to myself, giving only to those I call my friends and family, one touch, one smile, one glance from a complete stranger has me coming apart at the seams.

With a deep breath, I shove my disconcerting, wild attraction deep, *deep* inside and open my arms to the empty dining room. "Take your pick of the seats. I'll be right back."

Chase drops a canvas bag in one of the booths, and glances over his shoulder. "You really don't need to get me a drink. I'd rather you get an ice pack."

"I need to open anyway. Plus, I'm making you the guinea pig. I'm introducing a new holiday flavor today, and you get to be the first taste tester. Scared?"

Chase lifts a brow, and the dimple comes out to play. "Terrified."

I flash him a grin, securing a black apron around my waist, then set to work. Coffee can be its own kind of design. Not to boast, but I'm more than decent at cappuccino architecture. I've nailed the maple leaf, an evergreen, and I'm working on an intricate snowflake design.

A spritz of nutmeg, cinnamon, and crème. Peppermint and big crystals of sugar to top it off. Things I've sort of melted into a new Christmas-in-a-cup coffee.

But when I look over my shoulder in the dining room, when I study him a bit, another idea shapes. His skin has a bit of toasted tan to it. Being in his arms didn't turn me to jelly because of his touch alone. He's woodsy. A delicious forest scent lives on his skin, like he took a bit of the trees around town and used them as his loofa.

Inspiration grows, and I add the thing Chase Thorn's coffee needs.

The scrape on my face still burns, but being in my kitchen creating new tastes always brings a bit of magic. Outside worries disappear. Stress melts away. By the time I return to the dining room, Chase has stripped his coat and has a laptop and thick book settled on the table. I'm curious, but it's not my business to ask what it's all for.

I don't usually wonder over my customers. Even ones I don't recognize, so I'm not sure what my head is doing here.

I hold up the tray to hide the ping pong match of thoughts about Chase Thorn bouncing in my head. "Ta-da! Jeri's unnamed specialty is yours to enjoy. And critique."

His mouth twitches. "I'm not going to critique your coffee."

"Why not? How will I know if it needs to be improved if no one says anything?"

"You like criticism?"

I shrug. "Stings a bit, but without some pushback how do we change? I'm not worried, though. It's going to be amazing."

He laughs softly and picks up the white cup. They're the cutest little cups with black profiles of Christmas trees on the side. Snagged them on a deal last year, and I've been waiting since Halloween to put them out.

Chase watches me from over the rim. Okay, maybe I should leave. I don't really want to know if he hates it because I like his sexy face and I'd hate to have a reason not to. But I'm addicted to the first reaction. It tells me a lot, and as I said, it helps me improve. I'll know in about a second if there is something off.

He slurps. Doubtless to dramatize the moment. Coffee, crème, spices hit his mouth.

For a split second I'm jealous of a hot drink.

Oh—brow lift. Small smile. A second sip. I almost jab my fist in the air like Rocky Balboa. I think we've got a win.

"Wow," he says, inspecting the cup. "This is really good."

"Yeah?" I slide onto the other bench, inviting myself into his space. This is important market research and feedback, though. He'll need to understand. "Why?"

"Why is it good?"

"Yeah. What do you like about it? Describe it to me."

"Uh, well, I guess I like the spice with the sweet. And the sugar crystals were a good touch."

"Thank you, I thought so, too."

He grins and my legs sort of wobble even while sitting.

"And the crème wasn't too much to hide the cinnamon and . . . what is the other flavor?"

"The original only had crushed candy cane, but you gave me another idea, so I added hazelnut."

"Huh." He looks at the cup again. "Wait, you added a new idea to your already made-up drink just now?"

"Yeah. You give off a hazelnut vibe, so I trusted the old gut. If you're not lying, I'd say it was right."

"I'm not lying," he says. "I'm impressed, maybe a little scared that you guessed my perfect cup of coffee by looking at me. It's really good."

"I know!" A little squeal squeaks out of my throat.

"To be honest, though, I think the best part is you."

This is the moment I die in a booth in my café. My stomach twists and I hate it. Stranger. Hot stranger, but stranger all the same. I'm getting caught up in the romance of the season. I'm a free spirit, the kind that lives for my people and food, and I don't need anything else.

"Me?"

"Yeah," he says. "Your reaction is making this so much better. You really like your coffee, I'd guess."

"No. I love my food. It's exciting to make something new and watch people enjoy it."

"You made up everything here?" He kicks his gaze to the chalkboard menu over the register.

"Well, yeah. It's my job to create fresh new stuff. I love it."

"And you find inspiration . . . where?"

Is it weird that I'm sort of loving how much interest he's taking in my process? No one ever digs deep. I think people assume I simply know how to make all the food and don't put much thought into delicate flavor balances, or textures, or presentation.

"Inspiration comes from anywhere if I'm open to find it. For example, a conversation between two grumpy guys. They'll argue politics, or about the reckless younger generations, so I'll come up with a plate of opposites. Maybe a new surf n' turf with chili sauce, or a coffee with savory and sweet."

"And me? I'm hazelnut."

Heat floods my cheeks. "It's what came to me."

"Wonder why."

He's fishing, but I'm absolutely not going to describe the smooth flavor came because I couldn't stop staring at his skin, or caramel eyes. Thankfully, the bell over the door jingles. I glance at my wristwatch. Ugh, five minutes after opening and I haven't flipped on my sign.

Clearly, people don't care.

"Jericho!" Pamela Tilby hurries inside. She brushes a few snowflakes from her beehive hairdo, and devours the dining room with her eyes before she finds me. "Oh, Jeri! *Jeri!*"

She practically moans my name she's so desperate to tell me whatever gossip is on her tongue.

"Excuse me," I whisper to Chase, "duty calls."

He winks. Geez, he shouldn't do that. It's black ice all over again.

Forcing my feet to keep steady, I wave. "Pam, good morning. The usual?"

Raspberry tea with a chocolate biscotti.

"Oh, yes. Please, yes." Pam plops onto a barstool, her oversized purse takes up half the counter. Truth be told, I'm a little surprised she hasn't noticed Chase yet. She's like a hawk in a storm, always snooping and looking for the next gossip path. She slaps her palms on the counter, making me jump a little. "Have I got something to tell you."

Chase opens the book, but he's grinning. Pam is a character. Always breathless, always ready to spread the news. If there is ever an emergency, we don't need an alarm system set up around town. We'd tell Pam and she'd get the word out.

"What's going on?" I add a bit of milk to her tea, and place the biscotti on a white plate.

Before she tells me, she takes a long gulp, and chomps off the end of her treat. "Marilyn came into the shop last night. Wanted a perm of all things, didn't work on her, but that is beside the point. She'd been talking with Christine Powers, who spoke with Nancy at the post office, who is Facebook friends with Loo Graham."

She draws in a long breath before going on. "I think Sloanie and Rowan are having a baby! Why didn't you say anything, being as close as you are with them? We need to throw a baby shower, Jericho! Do you know the sort of planning that goes into something like that?"

I bite the inside of my cheek, and wipe down the countertop. "Pam what are you talking about? Who said they're having a baby?"

"Well, like I said, concern went down the line. Abigail told Loo, who told Nancy, then went to Christine, who visited with Marilyn before she came into the shop, that Sloan has been falling asleep without warning *and* has an aversion to pine scent. Jericho it's Christmas! Everything is pine, and Sloan lives in the mountains. How can she have an aversion to our entire town?"

This woman must get exhausted by the end of the day. It just doesn't make sense how her brain can keep track of so many conversations, and so many theories all at once.

I know the truth, but it is my sworn duty not to tell a soul until the father of the baby is made aware by a cute Christmas announcement.

I've got this. "Pam, I think Sloan would've told me, and really it's not our business—"

"Business has nothing to do with it, Jericho! Things like baby showers take *time* to plan."

I steal a look at Chase who is wholly invested in our gossip now, sitting sideways in the booth, sipping his custom coffee.

"Pam," I say. "I'm not sure where the rumor chain—"

"Conversation, sweetie. Rumor is such a mean word."

"Fine. I'm not sure where these conversations are getting the details, but I haven't heard anything." I've never wanted to be a good liar more than I do in this moment.

"Hmm." Her shoulders slump, and she narrows her eyes. "I think I better go visit Sloanie and see for myself. I've always been able to detect a little one, usually before the mother knows. Oh, oh, and don't let me forget to talk with you about the tree lighting festival. We need to talk food and drinks."

I chuckle and abandon her when the forest service guys show up for breakfast. Of course she would think she has a right to question Sloan Graham. It's one of those quirky, annoyingly awesome things about Silver Creek. People care. Sometimes way too much.

I get lost in the rush of the morning. Breathing a little easier when Tayla, my ever-reliable barista shows up.

The new candy cane coffee is a hit, but only Chase sparked a different flavor idea with the hazelnut. As the rush slows, I think of taking a break. Maybe in his booth again. But when I look, he's gone. Tayla is there, cleaning the few dishes, and gathering a cash tip.

Disappointment hits like a fist to the heart.

Get a grip, Jericho. You don't know him.

Still, I can't exactly lie to myself because the truth is I wouldn't mind knowing him. For the first time in forever my ribs want to crack a bit and get to know someone on a different, cozier level.

And that thought is scarier than Pam's beehive.

Chapter Three

Chase

I came here for the slow pace. The refuge. My grandpa's old house was the perfect place to get a bit of solace and break through this blank spot in my head.

What I didn't expect was to have the busiest, loudest morning to rival those I lived daily back in Los Angeles.

When I asked Mrs. McGregor, my new neighbor, where I could find a good coffeehouse she promptly directed me to the Honey Pot. Cutesy name, but I figured it would be a place of hipsters on laptops, beanies, and a lack of interest in the world around them. A good place to warm up and be around living, breathing humans who might spark some kind of inspiration.

I didn't plan on getting caught in the World War III of snowball fights, nor catching a woman. A woman who snapped through a bit of my glum the second those sunny eyes found me. Did she know her eyes practically glowed? She must not or Jericho Hunt would be more careful with her glances.

And—plot twist—she owns the Honey Pot. Funny how things go sometimes.

My agent would tell me it's fate. I think it's more a mutual love of coffee.

The entire atmosphere of Jeri's place itched in the back of my head. Almost like my brain wanted to pull something from the reality of this town and twist it into something fantastical, yet relatable.

Almost like I had the beginnings of an idea.

From the booth I watched the gossip mill buzz around Jeri like she was the basecamp. Everyone wanted to tell her about their mornings, their evenings, their plans for the Fourth of July in seven months.

Strange, but I could've watched it all day. Something about my not-so-damsely damsel intrigued me. A risk, to be sure. I knew what happened when that spark of heat shaped in my chest. The attraction that might end in a feeling. A feeling that would end in heartache.

Doesn't matter. I'm not here to be social; I'm here to work.

But when work calls, I let out a groan as if she's interrupting something vastly more important.

The first call I let go to voicemail, and I start to work my way out of the café.

Jeri laughs over the counter with a rugged old man who obsessively strokes his wiry, peppered beard. Part of me wants to say goodbye, maybe ask her where I might see her again, in a casual way, of course. But I resist. Jaw tight, I pack up my station, leave a hefty tip, and escape into the chill of the late morning.

In the fifteen seconds it takes for me to abandon the Honey Pot, my phone rings again. If I keep ignoring it, she'll keep calling.

"Tasha," I say. "How are things in the big city?"

"They'd be better if I received consistent updates from my most elusive client! Are you dead? Starving? Frozen? I don't know because Chase. K. Thorn never calls me. Never even emails me, to be precise."

I roll my eyes and pinch my cell between my shoulder and cheek as I adjust my satchel. "Tash, we talked about this. The whole point is to disconnect from the world and write."

"Disconnect from social media and mother phone calls. Not your *agent* who is trying to keep a *lucrative* publishing deal, Chase."

This isn't the first time we've had this conversation, and I doubt it will be the last. I also hold serious reservations that my lack of checking in with my agent every week will be the end of my seven-book publishing deal. They've already published six of the seven; I don't think they'll stop now.

But I've known Tasha long enough to know there isn't a point in arguing.

"Noted, Tash. Listen, thanks for the call, but I better get to work."

"Right. Do that," she says. "I expect at least the first three chapters by the nineteenth. I refuse to read over Christmas, Chase. *Refuse.*"

My eyes pop. "That's in two weeks."

"Yep." She pops her 'p' to annoy me, no doubt. "Once upon a time, Rex Blade could bust out three, clean chapters in a weekend."

It's a stab to the chest. I don't need reminding that I'm losing my touch. My writing mojo. My reason for existing. Not to mention my livelihood.

Okay, now I'm being dramatic. The Rex Blade pseudonym has made enough money that Chase Thorn can live comfortably for a long, long time. But if I can't write, then what sort of contribution do I even give to society?

"Thanks for the pep talk," I say after a long pause. "I'll get on it."

She hesitates. "Chase, I know things have been tough lately. I really do get it. But life . . . it needs to go on, you know?"

My eyes squeeze shut against a dull ache in my head. "Yeah."

"Okay." She softens her tone. "Find the joy in the writing again and the words will start to flow. Trust me."

"You're right." I rub the bridge of my nose, looking ridiculous standing in the middle of the sidewalk. "I'll keep you updated."

We disconnect and a knot sinks deep in the pit of my gut. Two weeks. Three chapters. What once would bring me a thrill, the chance to dig deep into another world with rules, magic, and religions of my own design, now crushes my spine.

"Hey! Yoo-hoo!"

I glance over my shoulder. The stout lady from the café, the one with the Jackie Kennedy hairstyle, waves her hand and shuffles her feet on the walk, careful not to slip. She's beaming at me, and absolutely not dressed for winter. At least not modern winters. The woman is wearing a dress with a long coat, thick nylon stockings with the seam up the back, and tan pumps.

For a second I do a reality check to make sure I'm not imagining a character. Never happened before, but I've heard stories about authors slipping into that weird space where they can't decide what's real and what's not.

But when the woman comes close enough to give me a whiff of her flowery perfume, I figure I'm in the real world. I wouldn't pick that scent, the clothes, or the hair for a character.

"Hi. Phew, you've got a set of long legs. I wasn't sure I'd be able to keep up with you."

"Sorry, I didn't know you were trying to get my attention."

"Oh, I wasn't after it at first. Not until I saw your face and thought to myself, Pam, you don't know him. You best go get to know him."

"Ah," I say. I'm not great at conversations anyway, but this one has me ruffled. She's bolder than me. I've never been one who can simply go talk to another human out of sheer curiosity. I'm lucky I talked with Jericho at all, but that's only because she landed in my arms.

"Pamela Tilby," she says, holding out her hand. "I'm president of the community activities committee. Because of my position, I tend to know everyone in this place."

Going out on a limb, I'd say what she means is she knows *everything* about everyone.

"Pleasure to meet you," I say.

"You're Paul's grandson, the one he left the house to, right?"

My brows lift. "How did you—"

Pam snickers and waves me away. "Oh, everyone loved old Paul, rest his soul. A bit of a recluse, maybe a little grumpy there at the end, but you look a bit like him, you know. Plus, I know Aida who works at the city building, and she told me the cabin had been sold to another Thorn. You're too young to be his son, so clearly, you're his grandson." She takes a short breath, and barrels on. "Now, Mr. Thorn, what sort of plans do you have for the cabin? Are you staying in town? Renting? B & B? If you go the bed and breakfast route I have a few thoughts I could run by you, but you should know this is a small town, and we already have a delightful inn with well-loved owners. It could cause some strife, then again no one likes a monopoly. What—"

"No," I interrupt, my hands go to her shoulders. "I have no intention of running a bed and breakfast."

"Well, that's a bit of relief. Are you planning on living there? If so, what do you do for work, or are you planning on starting a business of your own?"

I'm not sure this woman even realizes how much she talks. It's sort of entertaining. Sort of intimidating too. "I, uh, I work at home."

She lifts a brow. "One of those internet guys? You know, writing that weird language that I'm almost positive has tricky symbols that make it so the government can spy on us through the web. It happens, Mr. Thorn."

I haven't moved, but feel as if I'm spinning. "No. I'm an author."

Her face brightens. "Oh, well, that's spiffy. Any luck with your books, or are you just one of those looking to hit it big?"

"I've done all right." More than all right, but it's tacky and dumb to brag. Especially to a woman who will hire a plane to fly over town with a banner that says, *Hey y'all, a rich guy moved in at 23 Black Bear Way.*

"Well, this is fabulous," Pam says. "We've never really had an author in town. Not a real one, at least. I mean, the ladies at bridge club and I sold a hundred copies of our hometown cookbook we printed ourselves. But *some* people don't like to give credit for it. You know it's hard being your own publisher, Mr. Thorn."

I grin and adjust my satchel again. "I imagine it's really hard. I wouldn't sell ten books if I didn't have someone holding my hand."

I must've said the right thing because the woman bats her eyes and puffs up at the praise.

"Oh! Wait a hot minute. I've just had the best idea. Oh, this is perfect, just perfect." Pam jumps on her heels; she grips my wrists, moving my arms as if I'm supposed to jump with her. "You can be Cookie Tinsel at the tree lighting festival!" She draws in a deep breath, a wide-mouthed grin on her face. "Oh, Chase. You are the luckiest find I've had all day. Say you'll do it. You will, won't you?"

"Uh, what is Cookie Tinsel?"

She snorts. "Not what, a *who*. Our jolly storytelling elf at the tree festival. The last three years it's fallen to Bruce Wansgard. He's a darn lumberjack at the mill, Chase. Do you think he knows how to tell a story to bring childlike wonder to the season?"

"Oh, thank you, but that's really not my kind of thing." I wave my hands, desperate to get away. I can write books—well, I used to write books—but telling a story face to face, not my thing.

"The children, Mr. Thorn." I stop retreating. Is she . . . *crying*? How did the woman summon tears that quickly? She rests a hand on my arm, chin quivering. "Think of the sweet little faces, so vibrant, so innocent. All looking for that one special person who can immerse them into a world of sugarplums, and magic, and snowfall. Without you, they'll be doomed to hear tales of Snippy the Squirrel, and the contest held at the lumber mill for the poor thing's head. He's still an outlaw, and it's practically a guarantee that Bruce will tell the poor little souls all about the updates on spiked nets, barbed wire, bullets, and gore. The *children*, Chase."

"Okay!" This woman is either insane or deviously skilled at persuasion. Maybe a bit of both. "Okay, I'll tell a few stories. A *few*."

She makes a little chirp and claps her hands together. "Wonderful! We have our first meeting tomorrow evening at the courthouse. Now, I hate to be rude, but I really need to be off."

She's halfway down the sidewalk, me, still a little stunned, when she turns around and waves. "Oh, and welcome to Silver Creek, Mr. Thorn!"

I'm not entirely sure what just happened, but I think I agreed to be an elf in a crowd full of people I don't know.

Noted—Pamela Tilby is to be avoided in the future.

I keep the lights in the house dim. Setting the mood or whatever.

Truth be told, it's a little unavoidable. Grandpa Paul's old cabin uses outdated bulbs and no overhead lighting. Time for a few can lights, or at the very least some LEDs.

The cabin is cozy and home to some of my most pleasant childhood memories. Every summer for four whole weeks, I'd fly away from the bustle of the city and spend it fishing, hiking, and hunting with Grandpa.

Stories around campfires spurred my love of creation.

Naturally, when I learned he'd left his old house to me, I thought it might be the chance to turn my downward spiral of dead-end ideas around.

I slump back in my chair and scrub my face. The blank screen of my laptop stares back, taunts me is truer.

I've been in Silver Creek for nearly five days and the only spark I had was at a café. And only because a woman I don't know has a laugh that seems to light up the room like the Christmas garland in the street.

Jericho Hunt. Jeri for short.

Quite a name. Interesting, too. I could picture it tagged to an assassin, one with a cowl and a single blade on her belt. One who kept to darkness, dancing through as if she could simply step from one shadow to the next and disappear. She'd certainly survive in high mountain caves, or maybe a forest with wicked trees and poisonous thorns.

. . . called Hunt because she was born a hunter, never the hunted . . .

I jolt up in my chair. Was that . . . was that a backstory? A freaking character mantra?

Before I overthink it all, I type out the first sentence. Then, for five minutes, without stopping, I jot down a few physical characteristics. Hair the color of pine needles—it'd help Hunt be able to stick to the dry trees, ravished with a magical blight that is shredding apart her wor—

I shake my head and delete the magical blight stuff. Too predictable. No, this character, she wouldn't be the chosen one trope.

The entire battle of this final book has been the challenge of creating a new character to play off my main character, Kage Shade. A beloved, morally gray king's assassin who ended the last book with a wretched cliffhanger and in a precarious situation.

So, who would Hunt be to Kage?

Thoughts of Jeri reprimanding—more like terrifying—half a dozen teenagers this morning shape in my head.

I chuckle and type out the trope for this almost-a-character: Antihero, love interest.

A favorite of mine. Gritty, unpredictable, sometimes dancing precariously on the line between right and wrong. This Hunt would be Kage in female form. That'd give him some conflict to manage, no doubt.

A grin twitches over my mouth. This day finally sparked *something*.

I hover my hands over the keyboard again and . . . nothing.

No, no, no. Come on. Massaging the sides of my head, I fight to keep the image, fight to keep immersed in my world. But once more, I'm stuck staring at the blinking cursor with nothing more than a bit of physical traits, a trope, and a name.

Progress.

Pathetic progress, but it's progress I guess.

I shut my laptop, and out of habit I check my phone for any life. As usual, the screen is blank. I don't know why I expected anything otherwise. It never changes. Moira, my sister, is too busy in her law practice to take notice that the world is spinning. My parents are probably at my dad's corporate Hampton retreat this time of year, and my fellow author friends, well, we're all introverts. We chat at book signings and the once-a-year trip to the middle of the country to write, drink, and discuss our works in progress.

I missed last year's. And the year before. They told me they understood, and hoped I could make it to the next one. But we don't talk much in between, and I don't know why that bothers me tonight. I'm usually fine on my own, but for some reason it'd be nice to hear another voice outside of my own head.

With a knot in my stomach, I unlock the screen and lift the phone to my ear. I shouldn't. Go talk to the neighbors, go into town, anything. Because this voice I'm after isn't healthy. Still, I ignore my own warnings and dial the number anyway. My chest tightens when it goes straight to voicemail.

Her cheery voice is a knife to the chest. *Heya, it's Heath. Hope you're having a great day, but make mine better by leaving your voice at the beep.*

I hang up before the tone sounds.

What is there to say anyway? She won't call back.

Chapter Four

Jeri

A smoky scent hangs in the air when I step out of the small market. It's the best place for coffee beans in town.

The walks are thick with people buying gifts, or scoping out the intricate window paintings Ava Dillon, our local artist, does each year as a gift to the businesses. Every sparkly scene brightens a bit of Main Street with Christmas magic. The market's window is a scene of Santa Claus and his elves on a runaway grocery cart. Mine at the Honey Pot is a miniature Christmas tree decked in lights, and a curious black bear sniffing a pot of honey in the snow.

I adjust the paper sack in my arms and head into the bustle.

"Jeri! Jeri!"

An instant smile cuts across my face. I don't know how the girl does it, but without fail she can find those she cares about anywhere.

Abigail weaves down the walk, her reddish hair in long braids over her shoulders, glasses askew, and new braces that make her look too old. She's about to turn twelve and I don't like it. I've known her ever since she was little, right after Rowan bought Holly Berry Inn and took over guardianship for his niece. She's starting to look more like the Graham side of the family, but there's a strong resemblance to her biological dad too.

Either way, Rowan better get ready for boys noticing his girl soon enough.

"Abs." I give her a quick squeeze. "What are you doing, girl?"

"Just some Christmas shopping. Oh, and guess what?

"What?"

Abigail leans in, checking over her shoulders. "I hacked my dad's phone. Totally changed his text settings so every time he sends a text to Grandma and Grandpa it says *fart* whenever he types *okay*. He always says okay in his texts."

This kid—she's something else. "Should we take bets on how long it takes for him to figure it out?"

"Two days tops."

"I'm going with one before he blows his mind."

Abigail snickers, but muffles it when Sloan comes up behind her, breathless. "Hey, Jer. Geez . . . you'd think I ran here. What are you two talking about?"

Abigail widens her eyes at me, and gives her head a little shake.

I smirk. "Just how devious your kid is."

Sloan links her arm around Abigail's neck, tugging her close. "I don't know why that makes me so proud." She turns her gaze back to me. "Where are you heading?"

"I have to go meet with the tree festival committee or Pam will hunt me down, and I wish it was a joke."

"But it's not." When Abigail starts talking with a girl from her class, Sloan takes a step closer, voice low. "So, uh, any sexy guys sweeping you off your feet today?"

My mouth drops. "What . . . oh, my gosh this town is insane. Who told you? For the record, I didn't get swept off my feet. I was pummeled off my feet."

"Abs heard some kids talking at school about hitting Miss Jeri, and how some guy saved her. Then the bunko club had their monthly lunch at the inn yesterday, and all anyone could talk about was the new guy in town, and how he made his debut at the Honey Pot."

"First, he didn't save me. Well, he did catch me, but that's beside the point. And he didn't spend all morning at the Pot. I gave him a coffee as a thank you."

"Hmm. I don't know, Nadine seemed to think he was there for you."

I don't care for the way my chest cinches. There isn't time for this sort of ridiculous, lusty stuff. "If he came for me, then he would've been around today. Haven't seen him since he drank his coffee and—get this—left like a normal customer."

"M'kay," she says, a sly grin on her face. "What's new guy's name?"

"Uh, Chase, I think." I don't think. I know. Chase Thorn. Golden eyes. Strong arms. Yes, I know his name.

"Hey, Mom, can Lindsey and I go sledding tomorrow?" Abigail interjects. The two tweens look at Sloan with cheesy grins.

"Fine with me once homework is done," Sloan says. "And not too late. Remember your dad is stopping by the next morning."

They squeal. Abigail has gotten so much better about schoolwork and meeting kids. Once a ball of anxiety, now she's a kid who is rarely without a smile.

I jab my elbow into Sloan's ribs. "When did the mom and dad stuff start? She called Rowan, Dad, a second ago."

Great. I've made her cry.

Sloan wipes one tear away, smiling. "I don't really know. She just started one day. Rowan feels like he needs to talk to her about it because Scott does stop in a lot, and he doesn't want it to be weird for him."

I wave my hand. "Scott gave permanent guardianship to Rowan. He knows who's raising his daughter. Don't get me wrong, I'm glad the guy is a positive, consistent figure in her life, but now *he's* the cool uncle. You guys are her parents."

"That's what I told Ro. I don't want to discourage it because let's be honest—she's my kid, you know?"

"Yeah. I know. No one loves that girl like you and Rowan, my friend. I'm a close contender, but if I didn't know you guys, I would never know you didn't pop her out of your body."

She lets out a long sigh, and checks to make sure Abigail is distracted. "Nope. I get that honor in a few months."

"You'll be great." I glance at my phone. "Hey, I've got to get going or —"

"Pam." We say her name at the same time.

With a wave and tug to Abigail's braids, I quicken my step until I break out of the bustle and make it to my parking meter just before the time ends.

The courthouse lampposts each have a lighted snowflake on the side and five Christmas trees fill the entrance. It's not a large building. A few county council offices, the DMV, the sheriff's office, and a courtroom that is rarely used for more than speeding tickets. The carpet could use some updating, and there is a constant musty smell. Unavoidable, since the building hasn't changed much since the last remodel in the eighties.

Voices trickle down the corridor.

I let out a groan. Nothing is more awkward when you're the last one to a meeting filled with people unafraid to call you out for tardiness. But I score a bit of luck when I enter the room and everyone is too busy chatting to notice little old me.

Pam is at the head of the table; Mayor Harold sits next to her. There's Beatrice, the craft store owner. Next, Crimson Hall from the sheriff's office, and Dash Ellis, the representative from the lone diner, sit next to each other bickering about something. They're both a few years away from forty, legacies—as in their parents were big names in Silver Creek—and everyone in town wishes they'd stop the banter and go on a date already.

Finally, in the far seat, Bruce from the lumbermill, stares at his hands and grumbles under his breath. Always the same crowd, the same committee, every Christmas. But in Silver Creek not many things change.

Except . . .

Hold on now—on second glance there is another head at the table. What poor soul got wrangled into this?

When Pam moves her beehive, all at once the tips of my fingers lose feeling like they've been soaked in the snow outside.

Seated next to the mayor is Chase Thorn.

No wonder no one has noticed me. They're entirely engaged in railing Chase with questions. Poor man looks a little pale.

I guess I stand in the doorway, mouth open, for too long because before I'm ready, his eyes lift and lock on mine.

Happy Christmas to me. Those eyes, I mean, they match the tint of the golden ornaments on the court's garland.

Why, tell me why, I'm letting a complete stranger have such an effect on me? Truth be told, it's worse than an effect. I think I'm allowing his scrutiny, shapely jaw, delightfully sexy smile to split me down the center, then stitch me up again.

"Oh, Jericho! Finally." Pam slides out of her seat and hurries over to me, paper in hand. "Here is the menu. Dash will see to the donuts and fritters, but you can handle the hot drinks and mini sandwiches, yes?"

It slaps me in the side of the head that I haven't looked away from Chase. Get a grip, girl. Then again, he hasn't exactly looked away either.

"Ouch!" I rip my arm away. Pam, she . . . *pinched* me.

"Well, excuse me, but you're not focusing, sweets. Now, hot drinks and mini sandwiches—can you do more than cocoa and coffee? We'd really like some tea. Possible? Asking too much?"

"Uh." I shake my head and study the list of suggested beverages. "I think tea is a little harder to supply and the bags would be an added cost."

She pouts her lips and studies her list. "Well, we'll discuss it. Come and sit down. Yep, right there by our handsome Mr. Thorn."

Gladly, Pam. Gladly. My face heats. Never have I been so grateful thoughts were private. I give Chase a quick grin, and settle into the seat beside him. "Hi, there."

"Hey. Meet any snowballs on the way here?"

A weird, strangled chortle slobbers out of my throat. It sounds like I might be getting sick. Horrifying.

But he seems to find it entertaining since I get a glimpse of his straight, white teeth. A smile on Chase Thorn is quickly, and oddly, becoming one of my favorite things. Add on a day's worth of scruff and I'm a goner. I bet if I touched it a shiver would jump up my arms.

Oh my—I'm a freak. I'm literally thinking of stroking a man's beard.

I cross my leg, trying to remain aloof, you know, the way strangers do. "Um, so what brings you to the table?"

"Oh, oh, Jeri, you'll love this. I know Bruce does, am I right, big guy?" Pam says with a wink at the surly lumberjack. He literally only grunts and sips straight, hard black coffee from his thermos. Pam points her smile back at me. "Chase is taking the spot of Cookie this year."

I start to snort a laugh again, then clap a hand over my mouth. My eyes flick to Chase. Poor, poor, Chase. "You're Cookie Tinsel?"

"Apparently," he says with an added sigh.

"Why?"

"He'll be perfect," Pam insists. "He's an author, after all."

"Really? That's awesome."

Chase shrugs. "It pays the bills."

"What genre? No, no, let me guess." I tap my chin. "Thriller?"

He shakes his head, the grin spreading. "Too much police procedure I don't want to research."

"Science fiction?"

"I'm not that clever with science. I write high fantasy mostly."

"Ah," I say, nudging his shoulder. "Well, good evening, Mr. Tolkien."

I get the experience—no—the privilege to hear Chase's laugh. Is it his real laugh? I don't know. But the sound is smooth and deep and brightens my soul.

"I'm no Tolkien, trust me."

"Well, either way, I love fantasy novels."

"Yeah?" He adjusts in his seat, and our knees brush. A bit of heat blossoms through my thigh, up to my belly. Chase studies me, then asks, "What do you like about them?"

"Hands down the world building. How authors spin a completely new reality from something stemmed in ours is fascinating."

A groove shapes between his brows. "What do you mean?"

"Well, for example—"

"You two can dig into this later," Pam says, slapping the rolled paper of the drink menu on the table. She's smiling, but there's a bit of shut-your-mouth fire in her eyes. "Although, I'm glad you're making friends because we could use you two young bucks' help with the setup and advertising and prep work."

Chase leans back in his seat, a finger raised. "Question. If Jeri and I are handling all that, what are you all doing?"

Good job, Chase. He's been here for, well, I don't know how long, but he's already barking out some impressive passive aggressiveness to Pam Tilby. It's a skill that took me years to master.

Pam tilts her head, smiling that loving, yet condescending grin. "Honey, we have businesses to run, and we are considered the oversight committee —as in, we oversee everything."

I raise my hand, but don't wait for her to call on me. "Um, Pam, I run a business too. It's called the Honey Pot. Each of you comes at least three times a week."

"We know," says Crimson. "But you close shop at three while the rest of us stay open into the evening. Plus, you've got this guy to help you."

"He probably writes during the day."

"Surely can't take all day," Harold says.

"You're right," Chase says blithely. "We're young and reckless. We've got all the time in the world."

Teach me your apathetic ways, master. I nudge his ribs, grinning. We touched, and I didn't explode in a burst of this growing want. Close, but I survived. Probably shouldn't touch him again, though.

"Between the two of you, I have all the faith in the world things will be ready," Pam says. "I'll send you emails on where you can pick up supplies. No worries there."

"Goodie," I mutter. Now, Chase uses his knee to jab mine. He smiles and keeps his eyes straight ahead.

"You know, maybe we could use Chase as a publicity draw," Harold says. "If he's a well-known author it could bring some out of towners. More wallets in Silver Creek means more money in our registers."

"Oh! Fabulous idea." Pam claps her hands together and beams his way. "You're well-known, right sweetheart?"

A deep red color paints his cheeks, like the holly berries in the table centerpiece. He rubs his hands over his thighs, voice soft. "I have a decent fanbase."

Ah, sweet. That's something a person with a blowout fanbase would say. He's modest.

"I just googled you," Dash says, wiggling his phone. "Got nothing."

Chase looks like he wouldn't mind if the ground swallowed him whole.

"Dashall," I say, firmly. "Rule three of tree festival meetings—no Googling other members on the committee."

"So not a rule."

Chase drags his fingers through his thick hair, causing a few longer pieces to fall over his brow. I'd like to brush them . . .

No, I would not like to brush them away. My hands will stay laced in my lap. Perfectly reasonable hands. Well-behaved and such.

"I use a pseudonym," he admits. "But either way my books aren't Christmassy in tone, so it won't matter. I'll tell the *Night Before Christmas* and call it day."

"A real classic," I say.

"Thanks, I thought so." He mimics my light voice without missing a beat.

It doesn't take much to realize Chase doesn't want people knowing the ins and outs of his writing. Maybe he's not that successful, after all. Or maybe he's crazy successful and doesn't want everyone ragging on him for money. Or maybe he writes erotic romance under a name like Mandy Shivers. Who knows, really. The point is there are likely plenty of reasons he'd like to stay anonymous.

I should've known better. Not in this town. This place is where anonymity goes to shrivel up and die.

"Oh. My. Gosh." Crimson rises from her chair, mouth open. "You are *not* Rex Blade. Dash doesn't know how to do a thorough search."

"We all can't be hacktivists, Crims," Dash grumbles.

True enough. Crimson is surprisingly adept at online shenanigans because of her former work in the Denver Police Department. Like her father before her, now she works for the local sheriff, but pretends she doesn't moonlight with the FBI as an internet crimes consultant.

"Your name comes up alongside *the* Rex Blade," she says. "You have a TV show!"

Bruce surprises the room and grunts out a reply. "The books have a TV show. A good one to boot too."

My eyes go wide and I face Chase. A scratch grows down my throat, and no matter how many times I swallow, I can't get rid of it. No. *No.* He is not the guy who builds a world so vibrant, so tantalizing I can practically taste the magic on each page. The guy whose TV adaptation is taking its sweet time releasing season two, so naturally I have to wait before even beginning the episodes! But it taunts me. Whenever I login to my Netflix account, there it is: *Wicked Darlings*, staring right back at me.

I was in the arms of Rex Blade.

He sat in my café.

My gaze jumps to him. If Chase wanted to be swallowed whole before, I think now he's praying he turns to mist and simply flitters away.

"Didn't know his real name was Chase," Bruce says.

"Yeah," Chase fumbles. "I've worked hard to keep it that way."

"A TV show?" Dash says. "What's it about, Bruce?"

"I'm on the second to last episode and—"

"No, no, no! Stop!" I plug my ears. "No spoilers!"

"A TV show?" Pam says, breathless. Her hand is to her heart she's so flustered in all her excitement.

Chase sinks in his chair. My mind starts whirling, then all at once it lands on an idea. He saved me, now it's my turn.

"Holy cow, we are so late!" I bolt to my feet, one hand under Chase's elbow. I practically tear him out of his seat. What am I doing? I don't know, but I'm going with it. "Chase promised to sign the latest book for Abigail Graham."

Pam looks at me, astonished. "But you . . . didn't know his name, so how could he—"

"It's getting late," I carry on, "and she'll be heading to bed, and I refuse to let him disappoint his number one fan. We'll chat later, okay everyone?"

Bruce grunts again. "Rowan ought to think again about lettin' a kid read adult fantasy."

True. I may have just painted Rowan and Sloan in a weird way, but desperate times.

"Wait! I'll give you a ride!" Pam says.

"No." I hold up a hand. "No. You all know how Rowan is about visits once he turns off the open sign."

"Whatcha talking about?" Dash lifts a quizzical brow. "The man runs an inn. Folks come at all hours of—"

"Gotta go." I give Chase a look. Maybe we have a mental connection because I swear he nods as if he knows I'm telling him to make a run for it.

And we do.

Not a run, exactly. But a very, very brisk walk out of the courtroom and out of the building. The second the frigid wind hits our faces outside, Chase breaks into one of those smooth, comforting laughs again.

"Did we just run from a bunch of fifty plusers?"

I snicker. "Minus Crimson and Dash—even if they act like it sometimes. But get used to it. In Silver Creek, if you're not on the run from someone at least once a week, you're not living right."

He slows his pace, face to the sky. Chase's smile is free. "Thank you. I don't like when people find out my pen name when they know my real name too."

Thank goodness he couldn't see my brief, fangirl brain short circuit back there.

"Sorry they found out," I say. "They won't let it rest, so prepare yourself. There are no boundaries in this town."

"I figured it would come out eventually." He shoves his hands in his pockets. "But I wasn't ready for that."

"Well, now that my evil plan has worked and I have you all to myself, I plan on pressing you on all the details for the next book. Then, all the backstories that no one gets to know."

He chuckles, but there's a touch of nervousness behind it. "It's okay if you haven't read—"

"Hush your mouth. I know you're not insinuating I haven't read a Rex Blade book. Kage, the king's assassin, is my book boyfriend, and Noah Hayden is the perfect cast choice for young Kage in the show."

Chase hesitates, then gives me a shy smile. "I stand corrected."

The longer we talk, the more the nerves from speaking with a famous author fade.

"You know," I say. "We ditched, but in truth we are the lone wolves responsible for this tree festival."

"Oh, you caught that too?"

"We probably should plan a few things. If you're not freaked out that I know your pen name *and* your real name, then I know at least ten ways to sneak into the Honey Pot after hours. Coffee and plotting? Sound good?"

"Sound perfect." He nudges my shoulder with his again. "And funny enough, something about you knowing doesn't freak me out."

Blood pounds in my head when he looks away for half a breath. Maybe he's as unsettled at this weird easiness between us as I am.

Chase opens one arm, grinning. "Lead the way, Jeri. And I do hope you let us break into your own café."

"Oh, you think you can write action scenes? Tonight, you're going to freaking live one. Buckle up, Blade."

"Gladly."

A breath catches in my throat.

Did I imagine he said that? I don't know. But I'm certainly not imagining his hand on the small of my back, the backflip in my stomach, or the way I'm starting to like Chase Thorn too fast.

Dangerously fast.

Chapter Five

Chase

When I said break in, I thought it was all playful banter. Jeri, in fact, took it to heart.

I shudder. Not because it's twenty degrees outside. No. I'm laughing. Jeri is lying flat on her back in the snow, hidden behind a bench on the sidewalk as headlights drift past on the road.

"The snow works as a concealer," she whispers. "The perfect tool for a thief."

"More like the worst. Footprints. Dark clothes against white."

She waves the thought away as she stands. "You're invited to leave my imaginary heist if you keep that kind of attitude, sir."

Jericho bends at the waist, does a quick check over her shoulder, then bolts to the side of the Honey Pot. I'm not sure what I'm doing. Freezing in the snow, pretending to break into a building, and I'm . . . having fun.

This could work. As a scene, I mean.

Kage, Jeri's favorite assassin, needs a love interest my editors tell me, and this could work with my new underdeveloped huntress character. He could have a battle of wits with her over . . . storming a castle, or something simpler. Maybe a highwayman stole Kage's favorite sword and the huntress promises to help him retrieve it if he will pay off her debt with the pub owner where the highwayman is currently staying.

Yeah. It could work.

And Kage deserves a little banter in his life. After Wilja, the courtier everyone thought would be his life's love, betrayed him to the enemy in the last book fans are ravenous for a bit of peace for a beloved antihero.

She was a foolish woman. Too feckless with her antics when I live for the shadows. However, you will allow me my vengeance on her, boy.

My breath catches. Did I hear him? I'm not insane, it's an author thing. Characters talk and I haven't heard Kage in *months*.

"*Chase,*" Jeri whispers harshly. She waves me to her.

I'm sure I look like a lunatic, crouched behind a bench in the snow, staring into the night. But my mind is reeling in potential ideas. What is this woman doing to me?

Good things. That's all. No need to overthink it yet. I heard Kage. I thought of a huntress. The sort of woman a brutal, seedy character could love, right? And a scene is actually shaping in my head.

After another car passes, I trudge as quickly as the six inches of snow will allow. My toes are freezing, my jeans are soaked from kneeling, sitting, army crawling. Part of me thinks I ought to be weirded out that I'm following around a woman I hardly know like we're cat burglars. But another side can't help but embrace this oddness and roll with it.

Maybe I don't know Jeri that well, but I'm man enough to admit I wouldn't mind getting to know her.

The woman is picking the lock with a set of tweezers and a bobby pin. Who wouldn't want to know that?

She takes our invasion a step further and slides the window open, then tucks her master thief tools into her coat pocket like this is an everyday thing.

"Okay," she says. "I'll need a boost, then once I'm in I'll help you up."

"Do you pick locks often? Or do you just carry your thief kit around for a moment like this?"

She winks, ignoring the question, and rests her palms on my shoulders. Jeri's body is pressed close to mine, shoulders to hips. My head spins, my chest twists. A coal of heat sparks through the haze I've kept around my heart for nearly two years.

Like a skein of sunlight through dark clouds, something inviting and enticing stirs inside.

Impossible. I resigned to remain numb to matters of the heart and attraction a long time ago. I've lived my resignation perfectly too. Until now.

"Chase," Jeri says, laughing. "Focus. We're on the final step. Up."

I give an awkward kind of head bob. I'm doing this. I'm breaking into a café. With its owner. Because it's funny, I guess. And it is. For the first time I embrace the ridiculousness of this moment, and laugh. My shoulders relax, and I lace my fingers together, allowing Jeri to step onto my palms.

On the first try she fumbles enough that she needs to encircle her arms around my neck. She's hugging me, one foot in my hands, the other still tip-toeing the ground.

We laugh and try to steady ourselves.

"Okay," she says against my neck. "Just boost—*ahh . . .*"

Jeri shrieks when I lose my balance and slam into the side of the café. She squeezes me tighter, and I can't say I mind in the least. I'm still gripping her propped foot, but drop one hand to her waist to steady her. When did we get like this? Her chest to mine, her laughter in the crook of my neck, my arm holding her close.

Jeri pulls back. Her white smile cuts into the darkness, but it fades the longer we stare at each other. She's inches from me. I could kiss her with hardly an effort.

But a twinge of guilt bites in my chest faster than the laughter began, and ruins the moment. I need to keep my head here.

I clear my throat, forcing a smile. "Ready?"

This boost goes smoother, and in another heartbeat, Jeri slithers through her open window. Something crashes inside, followed by her bright laughter. Her face pops into the window and she holds her hands out for me. It's really not that high for my six foot two height, but I take her hands anyway and leverage awkwardly through the window.

I spill out in the back of the dining room, right over the steel countertop with creamer and sugar and napkins. My fat foot knocks over one of the trays with plastic forks for her treats.

"Crap. Sorry," I say, watching the forks spill over the floor.

"Don't worry about it. That was hilarious. I didn't think you'd go for it."

I find my footing and brush off my shirt, plopping into the nearest booth. "You're one to talk. I'm not sure if you're secretly a criminal or—"

"The window was unlocked," she tells me with a gleam of something wild in her eyes.

"What?"

She pulls out her bobby pin and tweezers. "The window was unlocked. But we had to make it look cool, right?"

I groan. "So we did all that and we can't even say we broke in? I feel cheated."

She laughs and takes the bench across from me, brushing bits of snow from her hair. "Next time we'll go through a vent or something, I promise. I better be added to the next book, though, that's all I'm saying. A tavern wench who breaks into her own place every time. Make me eccentric, but fierce."

"I would if I could write anything."

My fists clench over my knees beneath the table. Why did I blurt that out? Fun as Jeri is, I don't know her. She knows who I am now, but what would happen if she gave up that little nugget of information? Fans have already waited for two years since the last *Wicked Darlings* installment. To hear not even a chapter is written—it could pack some damage in that punch.

But when I dare look at her again, there's no smile, no devious glare. Her face is soft. "What do you mean if you could write anything?"

"Forget it," I say. "A poor attempt at self-deprecating humor."

Jeri stares at me until I freeze in my seat. It's a bit of magic in the real world because I can't seem to look away from those brown eyes.

"Are you struggling with writer's block?" she asks, so genuinely, I think I might spill my entire life history in one vent session, right here. Right now.

"A bit," I say, rubbing my palms over my knees.

"You don't want to talk about it," she says. "Because you're embarrassed, or because you don't trust that I'll keep it a secret."

She can read minds. No doubt about it. She rescued me as if she knew I was ready to run and hide in the courthouse, now Jeri Hunt can read my hesitation like I've written it out on my forehead.

"Listen, it could be hurtful to fans of the series if they knew it'll still be a while for the next book. I'm writing it, though. I am."

"I get it," she says, without a hint of disappointment. She doesn't seem ready to tweet the truth or alert Bookstagram. She's not calling Pam Tilby to spread the word that I'm a letdown to thousands of people. Her eyes simply drift toward the kitchen door. "Everyone thinks my head is always spinning in new ideas for food, but sometimes—it comes up empty. I went an entire year where I rotated through old menus to make it seem like I was making new stuff, but really I was recycling."

Unexpected. This isn't something I talk about with anyone. But Jeri, I don't know, it's almost like, to her, this is expected in my line of work. Nothing to lose sleep over.

I scratch the back of my neck. "How . . . how did you find inspiration again?"

"I shook up my routine. Started cooking in places that brought inspiration. Colors and textures were always a thing for me when I was at culinary school. I loved presentation as much as I loved cooking the food. So, I'd head to the mountains in spring. I'd cook over coals and look at the flowers. Or I'd visit different farmers' markets and try new seasonings, new smells. I took risks, I guess."

"That's what I tried to do," I say, a little envious. "When my grandpa left me his house, I was positive it'd help shake things up since I—" Whoa. We're not going into the reason the writer's block came around. I'm already giving up too much. "I just mean this place was where I first got ideas. I thought it would happen again."

Jeri props her chin on her palm. "What do you mean you got your first ideas here?"

"When I'd come visit my grandpa in the summers we'd go camping, or fishing. He'd tell me stories, and I fell in love with the art of it. I started pretending there was magic in the forests, or trolls under rocks. Grandpa Paul always encouraged it. Even had me convinced for two years Silver Lake, you know up in the canyon, was filled with selkies."

"I can't really picture Paul doing that, but I only knew him for a few years."

"After he turned into the grumpy old man in the woods?"

She bites her bottom lip and it stirs my gut in a want I thought died long ago. "I'm sure he was just . . . tired."

I laugh. "That's one way to put it."

"But since you've come back, I take it you haven't had much luck. I doubt you'd look so distressed if you did." She presses the pad of her thumb between my brows.

I like the touch. A lot. Maybe I lose a bit of my wits because I take hold of her wrist, and draw her hand away, but I tangle my fingers with hers.

We don't pull away. We're not exactly holding hands, more curling fingertips together. But it's strangely intimate.

"I think those are wrinkles because I'm getting old," I say, lightly. I'm not old. Thirty-five, but the way I've lived in a cloud of sadness, my body feels closer to ninety lately. "But you're right. I haven't had much luck until yesterday."

Her face brightens. "Really? What happened?"

Am I going to say this? Looks like it. "You."

"Me?"

"I don't know what it was, but last night I was sort of replaying the morning. You know, the way I was a hero and saved your life—"

She kicks me under the table, laughing.

I smirk and tighten our fingertip hand hold. "It made me think of a new character. Maybe it wasn't huge, but I haven't had any connection to the world in months."

I choose to leave out how Kage talked to me a few minutes ago. I'm not sure her food speaks to her the same as fictional characters have a place in my head. We'll leave the author quirks for when we know each other a little better.

"I wonder how to keep building on that character, then," Jeri says.

She's staring off as if deep in thought. Like this matters to her. How long has it been since anything with my books felt like it mattered to anyone else? There are always fans, and I've stayed active on my Rex Blade social media to keep the connection, but it's different when the people who know Chase Thorn are interested in *him*.

We sit in a comfortable silence for a long pause. Finally, Jeri stands and heads toward the barista counter. "Well, Chase, we're going to get your mojo back. We'll find a way to spark that inspiration."

"You don't need to do that. I'll figure it out."

"My interest in this is purely selfish. Not because I like you or anything. I need season two of *Wicked Darlings* before I can begin season one. I *must* know it will continue, even for one more season. It's a thing with me."

I let out a loud laugh. She says things and I don't expect them. "Well, now the pressure is on. I actually have a meeting with the studio right before Christmas. I'm supposed to have three chapters to show them and my agent; reassurance that I'll keep lining their pockets. So far I have a working title and a character mantra."

Jeri leans her back against the countertop, her eyes locked on me, and I have the distinct urge to go to her. To touch her, and hold her as if she is a ballast in this haze I've carried day after day.

"Well, that's because you only met your muse yesterday." She gestures to herself.

"Oh, is that what you are?"

"I know, I know. You didn't want to admit that meeting me spurred some thoughts." She wiggles a finger at me, winking. "I get it, it's intimidating when you meet someone of such caliber as me that it draws out Darlings yet to be discovered, but it is what it is. We can't run from it."

I can't stay across the room from her any longer.

Hands in my pockets, I stand close enough she needs to arch her neck to look up at me.

"My muse, huh?"

Jeri swallows with effort. Her voice shudders. "Yeah."

"A big responsibility, Miss Hunt."

"I can handle it, Mr. Thorn."

I don't fully understand what I'm allowing to happen here. Returning to Silver Creek was meant to be solitary. A place to reconnect with the Darlings, their prose, their voices. To escape the loneliness and emptiness that consumes me in one of the most populated cities in the United States.

I didn't anticipate finding comfort—no—finding *peace* at a small table in the corner of a coffee shop. And not with a woman.

A woman, who with a single look, breaks through the frosty outer shell I placed over my heart the day I lost Heather.

Chapter Six

Jeri

Sloan: Gotta be honest Jer, I'm not happy about always finding out dirty details about your life through PAM! Who is this man you ran off into the romantic Christmas night with? Snowball Chase? Different guy? Who?

I snicker as I read the text message. She gives me no time to respond before another bubble swoops onto the screen.

Sloan: According to Pam, unnamed man is so handsome he'll reverse her menopause. That's a direct quote. If it's snowball Chase, then I approve. He sounds like a dream. But if it's some rando, then are you alive? Did you run off with a serial killer? Who is he? Because he'll have another thing coming if he takes away my sweet roll girl, you feel me?

The air is cold and my fingers are already numb. Instead of texting my reply, I go old school and call her.

"Oh, good. You're alive. I was going to hit feral pregnant lady levels in half a second."

"You—chill. I didn't run off with a stranger."

"Ah. Snowball Chase then."

"Yes. Somehow we both were manipulated onto the tree festival committee."

Sloan chuckles. "Okay, well, tell me everything. What's going on?"

"I don't know, we're . . . hanging out, I guess."

Heat spikes up my neck simply talking about Chase. I ought to be unsettled with how much control this guy has over my emotions. But I'm not, and don't want to process what that all means.

"Okay," Sloan says slowly. "So, do you like him, are you going to go out with him? I need more details than hanging out."

"It's not like we've sat down and worked out future plans. He's nice, he's a writer, and Pam's right—he *is* sexy enough to reverse menopause."

"Hmm. I'm liking this. Now, tell me if this part is true. Is he Old Paul's grandson? Because that little cutie of an old man could certainly be a bear. Hard to imagine he got close enough to another human to have children, if you know what I mean."

Old Paul was a grump. But can anyone blame the man? Is aging really all that fun? I think not.

"Yes, he's Paul's grandson."

Sloan sort of hums. "Weird, but I think I've met him before. I have this memory of hanging out with Rowan and his older sister. Jenny and her friends hung out with a kid who visited sometimes. I might be making it up, but I swear Jenny said it was Paul's grandkid who came for the summer."

I arch one brow. Small world, and even smaller town. It's possible. Sloan and Rowan both grew up here, and Rowan's older sister would probably be closer to Chase's age. If he stayed with Paul for several weeks during the summer, odds are he met some of the locals.

"I wouldn't doubt it," I say.

She's already moved on. "Next question—when is he coming over so we can give our stamp of approval? You know Rowan will insist."

"Rowan? Or you?"

"Details. Come over for dinner sometime this week and—"

"Oh, hey, Sloanie." I freeze in the middle of the sidewalk. "I need to get going. I'm at the Pot."

"Say no more, but I will be bugging you about bringing Chase up here."

"Noted."

I end the call with a smile. My stomach flutters in velvety wings when a delightfully handsome author is sitting on the bench out front of my café.

Another wonderous thing? He's jotting something down in a spiral bound notebook. Dare I say, he's writing the next saucy scene involving Kage Shade? I'd like to unscrew the top of that beautiful head of his and watch it work.

Chase is fast becoming my favorite face to look at. The studious groove in his forehead, those thoughtful eyes. The way he rubs his lips together when he's thinking. Last night—truth be told I can't remember when I laughed so hard. Who breaks into their own café? Me, apparently. But I'd do it again if it led to the late night conversation we had over lattes and my homemade orange rolls.

He told me about living in the thick of Los Angeles. I told him about San Diego. We both share a love for theme parks and the ocean. There is a shadow of mystery in those eyes. But, funny enough, I hope I get the chance to crack the case of Chase Thorn. For the first time in what feels like forever, I'm not worried about being too busy, or too uninterested in letting another person into my tight-knit circle.

I like the idea of adding maybe one more, so long as it's this guy.

He intrigues me. He's soft spoken. The man understands the quirks of a creative brain. Bottom line is I like him. I liked him from the second I caught him scolding the kids on my behalf.

Maybe some of the magic in his books lives in him, because the last five dates I've taken the time to go on, I overthought every little thing the guy did. That, or I spent most of the nights mentally planning menus, or thinking of the next day of work. I know—romantic, right?

But last night, the only time I thought of food was when I busted out the orange rolls. I never disengaged from our conversation. Never wanted to. I draw in a cold breath through my nose, a little smile teasing my lips. Something is happening, and, honestly, I like it.

He's so engrossed in his writing that he doesn't notice me. I bend at the waist behind him on the bench, and draw my face close to his ear. "Hello, my fellow felon."

Chase jolts, dropping his pen in the snow. When he registers my face, he lets out a breathy laugh, hand to his chest. "Woman, I'd like to see thirty-six."

With a smile, I nod my head at the Honey Pot, silently inviting him inside. He follows, and naturally takes up the job of opening shutters and shades without being asked.

"So," he says, scrubbing his hands together. "Where do I sit that's out of your way?"

"The house is yours, Mr. Thorn. Sit wherever those creative juices will flow best."

He pauses, and his eyes cut into me in a way that prickles the same rush of attraction through my chest. *Chill out, Jeri. He's thinking, not ogling. You're the ogler.*

"I'll just, uh, I'll be the lurker in the corner, I guess." Chase points to the back booth.

"Good." I pat his shoulder, beaming. "What'll it be Mr. Blade?"

"My coffee, no question." He leans in. *Oh, goodness.* His lips brush the curve of my ear. "Extra hazelnut."

From the crown of my head to the tips of my fingers, my body is awake. I shake out my hands, bury my disquiet under a smile, and give him a lazy salute. "Be back in a sec."

I set to work in the back, a little relieved to get a step away from Chase. Not because I don't want to be close to him, it's more that my head is spinning, and I'm not sure I want it to stop.

The bell over the door dings the by the time I come out with Chase's coffee and a croissant breakfast sandwich even if he didn't ask for it. Rex Blade needs to build worlds in the back booth, and that means nourishment for brainpower.

"Be with you in a second, Alan," I say to one of Silver Creek's bus drivers. He never skips his coffee—says it helps him survive the drive.

Chase already has his laptop open, the notebook at his side. His hair is wavy, a little damp from the few snowflakes that melted. It's the sort of hair perfect for running fingers through. I don't because I do have some self-control. I wish I could say the same for my thoughts, but at least those are private.

"Happy writing," I say with a wink.

Chase lifts a brow. "This looks amazing."

"It is. Perfect food for writing a vulgar assassin."

With a quick smile, I leave him and beeline it for the counter now that some of the city workers have shown up. And Alan is still patiently waiting.

Chase intrigues me to the point of vulnerability. The soft looks, the smile, the kindness in his eyes, all of it leaves me unafraid of cracking my chest and letting him see inside. In truth, the more that I think about it, with him, I almost want to.

By the time three o'clock rolls around my feet are aching, and if I went the rest of my life without creating another maple leaf on a cappuccino, I'd die happy.

I rub the back of my neck, placing the leftover food in the walk-in fridge. When I step out of the massive thing, I smash into a firm, delightfully broad chest. My fight or flight instincts have always leaned toward fight. Without much thought, my fists gear up, but Chase's hands land on my elbows first.

"Easy, killer. Sorry, didn't mean to sneak up on you. And, yes, I invited myself back behind the counter."

I rest my hands on my hips. "Are you telling me you ignored the employees only sign?"

"Yes."

I laugh, pat his chest over his heart before I think better of it, and head for the registers.

"But I plan to be an employee for the afternoon," he says, following me. "What do you need me to do to help you close up shop?"

"Oh, don't worry about it," I say and wave the thought away.

"No. You let me take up one of your tables all day long. It's the least I can do."

"And?" I open the drawer to the register, and dig through the cash.

"And what?"

"Did you get anything on paper?"

I flick my eyes to Chase, and my stomach twists in a delightful swoop when his jaw pulses with a shy grin.

"I have an outline for chapter one," he says softly. "And two thousand words written."

The cheer comes outside of my control. A real, genuine sound of pleasure and excitement. My arms take on a mind of their own and curl around his neck. I bounce on my toes, hugging the man, hardly caring that I'm so overjoyed for him I've now touched him entirely without permission.

He doesn't seem to mind. The laugh rumbles from his chest, and I feel it in my blood. Chase scoops his long arms around my waist and hugs me back.

Then, I realize what's happened. His heartbeat is pounding against mine. His skin is warm and inviting. He smells like the crispness of the forest. My fingertips tease the waves of his hair on the back of his neck.

Our noses are half an inch away, breaths a little shallower, a little rougher. Chase's smile is gone from his face, but a bright gleam is in his eyes. One palm gently rubs my back. He studies me. What is he thinking? Does he ramble on in his head about how a few days ago we didn't know each other's names, now he has me in his arms? Or am I the only one who's freaking out about this?

I've stepped wholeheartedly into a whirlwind.

Maybe it's simply friendship. Yeah. We're new friends. I want to help him break this block, and it seems to be helping. It doesn't need to be more just because he's a man and I'm a woman and there is an undeniable spark of chemistry surging between us in this moment.

Chase's eyes drop to my lips.

I understand completely. I've stolen no less than three quick glances at the fullness of his. Man, I bet they're soft, and I bet he knows how to use them.

Chase's hands gently slide away from my waist. He clears his throat and steps back, and I feel emptier for it.

"Thank you," he says, voice rough. "Thank you for being supportive. I don't know what I did to deserve a friend like you, but I'm really grateful."

Friend. There it is. Spread out in the open. I knew it. Should've believed it.

Chase and I are new, adult friends with a shared interest in creative outlets. True, he's closer to millionaire with his creative outlet while I'm smack in middle class in a small town, but creativity doesn't look at bank accounts.

I'm glad we're friends. Really. I even flash him my best, we're-new-besties smile.

Then, once I step back to finish closing, when Chase takes up a broom and heads out to sweep the dining room, why do I feel such a sinking, tight disappointment deep in my chest?

Chapter Seven

Jeri

For five days in a row, Chase has perched in that back booth. He stays there from open until close. The most appreciative customer, to be sure. Then again, he's the only customer I feel comfortable experimenting new flavors on. So far—I think I've nailed his pallet aura. Hazelnut coffee, huckleberry puff pastries with a hint of saffron. Caramel and Irish crème hot chocolate. Winter berry salads with poppyseeds and pomegranate.

I smile as I flip the switch on my open sign the second three o'clock hits.

Drew Phillips, the local pharmacist, laughs, arms folded over his chest while he shoots the breeze with Chase. I don't know what they're relating on, but the magic of Silver Creek is even with differences somehow the people here find something to love about everyone.

Even Bruce who says five words a year.

It's sweetly satisfying to see Chase settle in like he's part of the crew. Makes me look forward to getting to know him for a long time to come.

Makes me think other things, but friends, remember? We're friends.

Then again, Sloan was Rowan's bestie when they were kids. I close my eyes as I shut one of my shades. This inner dialogue—the kind where I try to justify all the reasons being friends with Chase isn't enough—needs to stop.

I know where it goes with a man in his position. Wealth, status, talent like his leads straight down to heartbreak town.

I'm not opposed to romance. But when you've been burned before, it's hard to peel back those scorched edges and try again.

When Drew leaves, the café is quiet. My fingers tingle in a bit of numbness when Chase does his thing of helping me sweep and wipe down tables. We're starting to fall into a routine, and it's nice. As many people as I love, there are times when life can be lonely. But Chase is slowly changing that.

"Ready?" I ask.

"No," he says, returning the broom to the little nook in the kitchen. "You won't tell me what this secret outing is, and I'm not sure if I should be afraid or not."

"I would be afraid if I were you." I wink, slinging my messenger bag over one shoulder.

The day is surprisingly warm. Even some of the recent snowstorm is melting away into slush and puddles.

The way Chase spent a good portion of today with a divot between his brows, it doesn't take much to guess he needs a change of pace to shake up those creative juices. I know just the thing, but can't deny it's a little nerve-racking. Not everything that works for one person will work for another.

Maybe he'll think this is an amazing idea.

Maybe he'll think it's stupid.

"Jeri?" Chase's voice cuts through my daze. He smiles at the door, holding it open. "Coming?"

With a nervous smile, I button my coat, and head into the afternoon stillness. The streets have a few lazy cars driving past, a few Christmas shoppers and skiers in town from the slopes, but mostly the town is quiet.

At my side, Chase draws in a deep breath, puffing up his chest. "I thought I'd hate this, coming from L.A., but it's nice. The quiet. The fresh air."

"I felt the same when I moved here. Although, on really cold days I miss the beach, and tend to hole up inside my apartment. Last year, I pretty much resigned to hibernate."

He laughs and pauses at the crosswalk.

A shiver runs the length of my spine when Chase's hand rests on the small of my back, giving me a little nudge to jog across the street in between cars.

"Where to first?" he asks once we cross.

"Jones Market. We're going shopping."

Chase offers me a bemused look, but shrugs and keeps up.

We park our separate cars next to each other five minutes later, but everything in the main square of Silver Creek is close.

The market is a quaint little grocery store with a corner filled with exotic flavors. Dragon fruit. Ghost peppers. Blood oranges with the perfect hint of sweetness. Ralph, the owner, likes to get a few weird sounding things, then place them next to his apples and celery.

Chase studies the market, as if it's the first time he's ever stepped inside one. Probably confused why I'm grocery shopping with him, but this is when the fun starts.

"Okay," I tell him, grabbing a shopping cart. "We're going to follow our gut in here. I'm going to look around, take from the vibe of other customers, the weather, anything."

"Okay," he says, hands in his pockets. "But what are we doing?"

"This plan has three parts, Mr. Blade—yes, you will be Rex Blade for a second. We're gathering. Studying people, finding our marks, following our gut. Just like Kage Shade would if his mark were . . . I don't know, hiding out in a market square at the base of the palace."

A gleam brightens his eyes. He's either thinking I'm nuts, or he's about to kiss me because of my brilliance.

I prefer the latter. One thousand percent.

Friends. Friends—ugh, that's turning into such a dirty word.

"You, Jericho Hunt, never cease to surprise me." Chase scrubs his hands together, tongue out one corner of his mouth, and scans the modest shelves. "Okay. Let's go."

I figured this would kill two birds with one stone. Chase churns his storyline, and I get my shopping done for dinner.

What I didn't anticipate, was rib-splitting laughter when I shouted at Chase to tuck and roll, as if a real assassin were about to charge. It took him half a breath, but soon enough, Chase went boneless. He sprawled behind the onion and potato shelves, made weird hand signals, I pretended to understand, and we both ended in a crouch behind the oranges.

He leans his forehead against the stand, face red, laughter squeaking out of his throat. We've drawn a few confused eyes, but basically those gawking people are now enemies of Kage, even if they don't know it.

"This is the weirdest thing I've ever done," Chase admits.

"But is it working?" I whisper back.

He hesitates, then blinks his gaze to me. The softest smile crosses his lips. "Yes. I'm seeing the world again."

Holy Christmas season, I want to kiss him.

I pat his shoulder instead, and slither one hand over the stand and snag a lime from a small box. "Good."

I run the lime under my nose and breathe it in. The sunshine, the laughter, my head starts spinning with something fresh. Something with a tang.

"You're doing it too," Chase whispers.

"Doing what?"

"You're imagining something." Chase drags a finger down my knuckles. My heart leaps to my throat when he smirks. "You twitch your fingers whenever you're coming up with something."

Do I? No one has pointed it out. I guess no one has ever paid attention long enough to really notice.

I smile through a flush and tuck the lime in the shopping cart we have unstealthily dragged with us through our fantastical escape in the produce section. "Must be the company. Ideas are flowing."

"They are." The way he says it, I'm not sure he's talking about books or dinner.

"Well, we should get the rest of the goods for my remarkable idea. Then, we'll move onto part two. We've got to be done with my grand plans before seven."

He groans. "Do I really need to go to a fitting? I mean, is it that big of a deal?"

"Yes. It's a big deal."

He staggers back to his feet, helps me out of my crouch, laughing when I announce my foot has fallen asleep, then we finish our shopping.

"Should we just take one car?" he asks, pointing at our two cars. He drives a Tesla—it's probably the only hint that he's spent a bit of money—but it's not so flashy that my little Toyota looks like a dump next to it.

"It'll be easier," I agree, but the truth is, I'd like to keep the good mood of this afternoon going.

He helps me load the groceries, then takes the passenger seat of my car, and looks more relaxed as we head toward the inn than I've seen since we met.

Part two: invite Chase Thorn to my house, cook dinner for him, then eat said dinner while discussing his thoughts on his outline.

Really my house is the guest house behind Holly Berry Inn. But there are two bedrooms, and a huge kitchen. I don't need much else. Inside, we fall into a dance around my place. Chase talks about his favorite foods as he sets the table, then asks me the strangest foods I've tried.

"Pickled pigs' feet," I tell him as I finish the final touches of spices in the skillet. "Not as bad as you'd think."

He grins, then sneaks a piece of the chicken straight out of the pan, laughing when I swat him with my spoon.

The day, the company, the mood, it all led me to create a lime chicken with zest and asparagus.

"Jeri," Chase says in a groan, rubbing the bridge of his nose after his first bite.

"What's wrong?" Panic hits hard, like a fist to the chest. He hates it. Okay, I can handle criticism. I grow with criticism. Still, I'm a little surprised. I was certain I'd been right on with my instincts.

Chase shoots me with a villainous kind smirk. "Not to freak you out, but I'm pretty sure I'm going to propose to you in five seconds. This is amazing."

I pitch a laugh. "Well, the feeling is mutual, Mr. Thorn. Get to *The End* with my favorite assassin, and I might kiss your feet. Speaking of my friend, have you ever thought about him standing up to the king?"

"In what way?"

"Well, he's the king's assassin, and they're weirdly friends. But the king is so morally gray, he rivals Kage. And King Lux suspected Wilja's betrayal, but said nothing. I don't know, I think Kage should let loose on him. Maybe tell him he's a total tool."

"Don't you think a king would punish a subordinate, though?"

"Absolutely. But will he? Lux loves Kage as a brother of sorts, but his own upbringing and arrogance makes him a bit of jerk, right?"

He nods, unbothered at my suggestions, and content with his food.

"Well, I wouldn't mind my guy standing up for himself. Something snaps inside maybe. It could be a cool conflict. Maybe Lux punishes him and tosses him into the dungeons, then wrestles with the dilemma."

Chase eats silently.

Maybe I overstepped. I'm a reader, and this guy, he knows every personality trait of his characters. I mean, the books are written from five points of view. How he splits himself into so many different voices I'll never understand it.

"Sorry," I say. "I talk like I have any idea how your story is going to progress."

"Don't apologize," he says, meeting my eyes. "I love when you talk to me about this. Sorry, I get quiet when I think." Chase leans back in his seat; his fingers drum the table. "You give me different perspectives to think about. This will sound weird, but your suggestions and ideas, they get me to check in with the characters in a way. Ask them if that's what they would do. Weird, I know."

"Not weird," I say. "Your characters might not be physically real, but you're still connected to them. I think that's why they feel so real to your readers."

"I like your suggestion," he tells me. "I think it might be an idea to explore a bit."

I sit a little straighter. "Well, glad I could help."

"I feel like this is all a take relationship here. I keep taking from you and haven't really given back."

"Not true." Am I going to admit this? Apparently—because my mouth keeps moving. "Lately, you're the only one who . . . triggers new ideas for me."

Chase leans forward on his elbows, pointing at his cleaned plate. "This?"

"Your laugh." What am I saying? In so many words I'm telling this man I like him. I'm on shaky ground here, unsure if it's all about to crack. "Um, that came out wrong. I just mean at the grocery store—it was light, and fun, and we laughed. So, this is a little sweet, a little sassy, and—"

Chase rests a hand over mine, and I stop rambling, lifting my gaze. There's a bit of relief when his expression looks as nervous as I feel.

He rubs his thumb over my middle knuckle. "You inspire me too."

In my belly a flutter of nerves boils until my heart won't stop racing. His eyes simmer in a dark, coal black, and they haven't dropped from mine. This is a moment—one where the world outside quiets until it's only me and Chase and the pressure of something seductive building between us. Inches away, and all at once I have every intention of kissing this man.

My phone alarm blares a shrill chime.

I'm startled enough I let out a shriek. Eyes locked on the screen, curses reel through my head. "Uh, the fitting. We . . . need to be there in ten minutes."

"Right." Chase lets out a long breath, chuckling nervously. "Can't wait."

Avery Henderson is an old seamstress with more wrinkles than icicles on her overhanging roof.

She's as sweet as cherries, though. The sort of woman whose entire face scrunches when she giggles. And she takes a great deal of pride in her work. Since Chase is taking over as Cookie Tinsel, the costume will need to be adjusted down from Bruce's broad, thick body to Chase's athletic figure.

He stands in front of three full-length mirrors like a good sport. But he's making it a real pain in the backside not to laugh. Avery can hardly hear, but I don't want the sweetie of all sweeties to think I'm laughing at her effort.

Chase keeps making faces in the mirror, pretending to be stuck by one of Avery's pins, or like he's an English gentleman taking tea.

Might as well be.

Cookie dresses in a fine blue waistcoat with gingerbread man buttons, a satin vest, and ruffled shirt. His pants are about as tight as stockings, and the curled shoes are flocked in bells with red sparkly balls.

Chase looks ridiculous and sexy in one glance. The coat shows off his trim waist, and the tight pants hug the muscles of his lower half in the best ways. Unashamed, I've checked him out at least five times.

"I saw that," he whispers, eyes on me in the mirror. "Keep your eyes up, Miss Hunt."

I'm officially the worst at being sly. Shoulders back, I lift my chin. "It can't be helped Mr. Thorn. I have a thing for elves."

He laughs. "Good to know."

"There we go," Avery says in her soft, trembling voice. "I think we have all the pins." She pats Chase's arm. "Take it off slowly."

He gives her a nod and hobbles to a dressing shade. Avery jots down her measurements, and by the time her arthritic fingers finish, Chase comes out, dressed in his clothes again.

"Hmm," I say, pouting. "It's just not the same."

"I can put it on again, Jer." He jabs his thumb over his shoulder at the costume back on Avery's mannequin.

"Tempting."

I hold my breath when Chase comes closer and helps me slip into my coat. His front is to my back. When his hands linger on my arms for a few heartbeats, I fight the desire to lean against his chest. Whatever is happening—this new flirtatious back and forth—it's spinning me in a delicious cyclone. I don't know what to expect, I don't even know what Chase plans to do here in Silver Creek.

But each day we spend time together, I can't deny my heart wants to fall for Chase Thorn.

And it wants to fall hard.

Chapter Eight

Chase

Not even my own mother makes me feel like an adolescent the way Pam Tilby does. The woman has one hand on my arm, the other on Jeri's, and drags us toward the old Main Street square like we've misbehaved, and she's going to give us a piece of her mind.

Jeri leans back, peeking out from behind Pam's beehive, and it's like I can read her mind. *Should we run?*

I give a quick shake to my head. *I don't dare*

Jeri beams, and my chest tightens in the new, hot pressure I keep experiencing whenever she smiles, or laughs, or talks. It's nothing, and I should stop making it something. She's a fun, new friend. Beautiful? Funny? Intriguing? Yes, but it doesn't mean the rush of blood or dry mouth are because I want anything more than friendship.

An image of Kage rolling his eyes at me forms in my head. A little gift from my subconscious that even my fictional characters don't believe me.

The assassin has been taking shape the last week in a brutal, exciting way. My little bench in Jeri's shop has helped unlock our connection again. Now, though, his grumbly, take-no-nonsense voice crops up whenever a glimmer of inspiration comes. Around Jeri—well, it's like I have two personalities. For some reason, she pushes away the fog and has a way of bringing clarity. I've had more new ideas since we met than the last year combined.

Even now, with Pam pulling me toward doom, I imagine Kage facing something similar. Something light, with a bit of humor to lull readers into a false sense of security before they're sent spinning into conflict.

A disgruntled mother, perhaps, who catches him in scandal in her loft with a daughter.

I would never be caught.

True. He'd move quickly. Unless the woman is surprisingly nimble and sly like Pam Tilby. One minute you think you're safe, the next she's dragging you toward the beginnings of the setup of a tree festival.

Could be an entertaining scene.

I make a mental note to explore it tomorrow when I'm in my warm little corner at the Honey Pot. Maybe I'll ask Jeri her opinion. I've never talked much about my plot developments with anyone but my editor. Still, the more the idea settles, the more I like the idea of having another head to bounce ideas around on.

"Do you see the problem?" Pam's voice shakes me from my thoughts.

We stop abruptly when she drops our arms, and shuffles to a little dais in front of the big pine tree that will be the MVP of the tree festival. On either side of the platform are smaller spruces, boxes of ornaments, and figures of different holiday characters from around the world.

Between all the trees is a gaping hole of nothing.

"What problem, Pam?"

Good. Jeri is as confused as me. Decorations are still being placed. Unfinished, but it's not due to be completely set up for the festival until next week.

Pam lets out a little grunt of frustration and points at the cluster of smaller evergreens. "Don't you see them? Jericho we've been invaded. We can't set up our Peace on Earth Christmas display until they're gone. And as members of the committee, not to mention you're both the tallest, it seems only fair that you take your turn ridding us of them."

"Of what?" Jeri asks again. "I only see the Scandinavian gnome has lost his hat."

Pam follows Jeri's pointed finger and practically shrieks, rushing to the hatless, bearded thing. "No. No, it's the trees. Those annoying magpies seem to like the cozy lights. They've taken over our branches and keep . . . well, I don't mean to be vulgar, but they keep *pooping* on the around-the-world Santas!"

Two things: Pam Tilby and I vastly differ on what we consider vulgar. Second, I'm not sure if I should laugh or run. We've been hauled in here to de-magpie trees?

"Pam!" Jeri props her fists on her hips. "You told me it was an emergency. I closed thirty minutes early!"

"Jericho! It is an emergency. Without our around-the-world display, does the message of Peace on Earth get told? No. It doesn't."

"But can't we all want world peace without a display? I mean, tell me honestly, shouldn't that be a year-round thing?"

Pam huffs. "It's Christmas, Jericho. We preach peace on earth."

"Very true, Jer," I say eyeing a black and white invader through the branches. The birds aren't even afraid of all the people standing around. "I personally only like to ponder peace for a few set days. It's really exhausting to keep it up all year, right Pam?"

"Exactly," Pam says, wholly missing my irony as she opens her hands in my direction. "At least one of you understands." The woman digs through some of the boxes and supplies around the dais. "Now, we've used shovels —to scare them not kill them, of course—and we've tried bags—"

"Animal control?" Jeri offers.

"Matthew is busy keeping the moose and mountain lions from devouring us, Jericho!"

"Ah. Then praise the man. Being devoured by a moose is the last way I want to go."

"It would make an interesting story, though," I say, giving her a look.

"True," Jeri goes on without skipping a beat. "And unforgettable funeral talk."

"You could add it to your headstone—first woman to be devoured by an herbivore."

"Ohhhh, that would be a conversation piece in the cemetery."

Pam watches us with a look of disbelief, maybe a touch of disgust. "Something is wrong with you both. Just . . . here." She shoves two canvas sacks into our hands. "I'm needed over at the food booths."

"But food won't be here for another ten days Pam," Jeri says. "You know, when the festival starts."

Pam is already on the move, but takes the last word over her shoulder. "There is never a better time to prepare than the present, Jericho."

Alone, we meet each other's eyes, muffle laughter, and face the trees.

"There is no way I'm going in there. Those birds are deceptively tame. They'll sit there and stare at you until they freak out last minute and attack your head. It's all wings and beaks, Chase."

I take a step to her side. "Where is Break-in Jeri?"

She grins and pinches my waist. "That was when I had control. These birds are unpredictable. We're calling in reinforcements. The big guns. A guy who's cleared out more bats from his attic than is humanly possible."

"Sounds intense."

She chuckles and pulls out her cell phone. "Sounds like Rowan Graham."

It's strange seeing Rowan after all these years. Last I saw him he was running around as an awkward fifteen-year-old whose body couldn't decide if it wanted to be bulky or skinny.

It chose broad and strong.

I'd been friends with his older sister. Rowan didn't spend a lot of time with us, but when he did he was always with a blonde girl.

There is something satisfying and heartwarming when the same blonde girl shows up wearing his ring. I have a distinct memory of Jenny Graham telling us that her little brother was going to marry the girl.

She was right.

Rowan arrived with his daughter Abigail, and her tween posse in tow. Jeri gave a hurried explanation about how Rowan stepped in as his niece's dad. I wish I could've been here for Jenny's funeral, but by the time I heard, they'd already buried her.

Honestly, it's a comfort to see her daughter so happy.

Not to mention, I'm surprised how the three eleven-year-olds actually help. They're calm as wings flutter and birds shriek. Abigail is swift on her phone, and pulls up a guide on how to de-bird a tree in a second, but soon enough we're not following directions. We're trying to survive. The girls laugh when I duck a rogue beak aimed straight for my eyes. Then, Rowan earns a glare from his wife as he curses loudly at two magpies charging the back of his head.

It takes over an hour. Closer to two, and by the time we're aimed at the last bird, I've been clawed at, pecked at, and the branches have left more than a few scratches on my forearms.

Our de-birding has drawn a crowd. Not a crowd who offers to help, despite having perfectly capable hands. But a crowd of people holding cups of coffee and cocoa, bellying up to the show.

"Ready?" Rowan asks me, a little breathless.

I give a stiff nod, grip my end of the canvas sack, and rush the tree.

The next moments are a whirlwind of powdery snow, wings, swearing, and a few jeers like the crowd is watching a boxing match. The wings brush over my cheek. The beak nips at Rowan's wrist. But in a few wild seconds we have the last of the birds safely caught and transplanted in several plastic totes Miss Wilma, an eccentric widow, uses to house feral cats in the winter.

Rowan wipes his forehead with the back of his hand and groans. "Now he shows up."

I follow his gaze to the silver animal control truck. A stout, balding guy steps out, adjusting his belt.

"Coulda used you Matt!" Rowan shouts.

Matt shrugs. "Sorry, man. I was caught up with the Whiner's goats. Got into the neighbor's yard again."

"So, *not* on carnivorous moose duty, Pam," Jeri grumbles.

"One of his many duties, Jericho," Pam retorts. The woman must always have the last word, I've decided.

We leave the gathering of the totes with the magpie family to Matt. Abigail and her friends follow, naming each bird and telling Matt where to set them free for their best quality of life. Proof children are more compassionate than me. I hate those birds.

"Well, that's one way to see you again." Rowan says, clapping a hand on my shoulder. "I don't know if you remember me, but—"

"I do," I say, finally holding out one bloodied, scraped hand. His looks the same when he takes mine. "I'm sorry about Jenny. I heard a couple months after she was gone."

He nods, a shadow in his eyes. "Yeah, it sucked. My mom still has your card, though. She kept everything."

I did send a big condolence package to the Grahams. Said it was from my grandpa and me. By then old gramps was already a little grumbly, but he did send me a couple bucks for the gift basket and told me what to say for him when I signed the card.

"Ah, look Sloanie. Rowan is starting to make more friends." Jeri slips next to my side. "He's not going to turn into the hermit you were afraid of."

Sloan grips his bicep and squeezes. "Even if he did, I still think he'd be a sexy hermit."

"Thank you," he says, pulling his wife against his body. "Jeri, pretty uncool of you getting Chase strapped into this festival."

"Take it back. I did no such thing. It was all Pam."

"Now I get it," Rowan says, glancing at me. "You're not officially part of Silver Creek until Pam Tilby wrestles you into something."

We laugh. It's strange. I've grown up with a big city life, visiting the mountains and small-town world a couple of weeks a year. But here, in this moment, it's like this is where I should've been all along.

Once Sloan and Rowan leave with Abigail and her friends, Jeri helps replace the figures of different cultured Christmas characters, then looks at me with a touch of mischief.

"Well, what now, Mr. Thorn?"

"What now?"

"How are we going to make Kage come alive tonight?"

I shove my hands in my pockets and take a step closer. "You really want to help?"

A splatter of pink colors the bridge of her cheeks. From the wind, or a sudden rush of heat, I'm not sure, but I like to think I unsettle her as much as she does me.

"I am always up for curing a severe case of writer's block. Again, selfish reasons. There is a TV show to think of."

"Of course. I'd never think anything less."

Truth is I'm not ready to say goodnight to Jericho Hunt. I wasn't ready when I watched the clock tick closer to three at the Honey Pot either. When Pam Tilby burst into the café at quarter after two insisting that Jeri close up for a dreadful emergency, secretly I'd been singing the woman's praises.

But I'm also not ready to dissect what it all means. Not ready to accept that I'm walking a dangerous line.

I shouldn't get close to Jeri. It would be a fierce betrayal to someone else.

Jeri dances around me, sort of like she wants to step closer, but isn't sure if she should. *She should*! My body is practically screaming for a bit of closeness.

I need to dip my head in the snow and chill out.

"Any ideas?" she asks, finally bringing the relief I don't want to crave, and coming close enough I get a breath of the honey scent of her hair.

"Yeah." I'm winging an idea. I take hold of her hand, and lead her toward our cars. "Come on. This should be interesting."

My idea is not going how I planned.

What *is* happening is a whole lot of cold and shivering.

Naturally, Jeri thought it was fabulous. Behind my cabin the forest slopes. A quarter mile up, the trees part, opening to the sky. In my head I thought: woods, darkness, stars. The perfect setting for a fantasy world. I forgot about the six feet of snow.

Leave it to Jericho Hunt to make a whim into something memorable.

She has tarps—I don't even ask—a camping cot, charcoal, and a Dutch oven in her trunk.

Now I'm huddled beneath a makeshift lean-to, a blanket around my shoulders, Jeri cozied up in her own at my side.

The glow of charcoal embers break the dark, heating something that smells amazing. A quick stop to the market and three bags of supplies later, Jeri has the same smile she wore when she created the hazelnut candy cane coffee the day we met.

"What are you making again?"

She pokes at the coals with a stick. "Don't know exactly. You mentioned a campout in the middle of winter, so I thought of Kage doing the same and it sort of . . . just came to me. I'm starting to like this mutually beneficial arrangement."

I stare at her for a long pause. She inspires me. No question there. But there is something deeply satisfying knowing I might do the same for her. Maybe I lose a bit of my mind, or maybe it's the need for more body heat, but I open one arm and drape my blanket around her shoulders.

Jeri draws in a sharp breath. She pulls her bottom lip between her teeth, unaware how the sexiness of it spins my head. With slow movements, she scoots next to me. Hips touching, knees knocking. Her palm falls to my thigh underneath the blankets. It's a gentle touch. Unassuming.

I can't get enough.

I *can't* go down this road. Not after I promised I wouldn't. But little by little, my fingers curl around hers. We stay like that for a few seconds, bodies close, and hands entwined.

"Chase," Jeri whispers.

"Yeah?"

"If Kage were here, what would he be doing?"

The corner of my mouth curls as I take in the trees, the hiss of whatever is in the iron oven, the slight whistle of wind in the branches.

"Complaining," I say. *Wouldn't you? What in the name of my gods would I be doing in the open forest?* I trace the shape of her knuckles, smiling at the moonlight. "He'd hide out in the shadows."

"What would make him run to the trees?"

I furrow my brow. A scene shapes in my head. If I go with the conflict with his buddy the king, Kage would run somewhere treacherous. "He'd only do it if the armies couldn't reach him."

She sighs softly. "I think so too. And King Lux, he has his fear of the highlands anyway because of his younger sister's death, right?"

A smile cuts across my mouth, and I tighten my grip on her hand. "Right. It could work. If Kage is on the run from the crown, naturally he'd go where Lux would have a harder time reaching him." I sit a little straighter. "He might save Lux."

"Oh, I like it." Jeri leans into me, excitement bright in her eyes. "Lux could be so angry at whatever lies or beliefs he's holding against his old friend, so he pushes aside his fear, all to go after Kage and confront him personally. Maybe he gets into trouble—"

"I've already written the Slate Cliffs into the landscape."

"Yes!" Jeri smacks my leg. "From book four! It's full of skulls, and Lux is totally inexperienced as an outdoorsman. Plus, it could really be a full circle moment."

"What do you mean?"

"Well, Kage is from the wilds of the place, it's where the first king rescued him from his cannibalistic family! Now the exiled assassin saves the king who wants him dead in the same place Lux's father brought the two boys together. Sort of poetic."

Reluctantly, I release her hand and pull out my phone. "Sorry, I need to write this down."

"Write away. Selfish reasons, Chase."

I grin and finish jotting down a few notes. "I think that's a lie you tell yourself. I'm starting to think you like spending time with me."

Jeri opens her mouth to respond, but stops. A curious little smirk plays with her lips, and I want to ask her what she's thinking. But she doesn't give me a chance before leveraging out of the blankets toward the Dutch oven.

I'm on thin ice waiting to fall in, but I can't seem to run back to the safe, guarded distance.

"Looks done." Jeri grins over her shoulder, lifting the hot lid with an iron hook.

I bury my disquiet and help her dish up.

"Chicken with a berry sauce, gravy thing. I don't know, pretend it's some random bird Kage caught."

I laugh and take a bite. It's a little explosion in my mouth. The woman is a surprising genius with food. A simple thought, a guess even, and she somehow collided the sweet and savory into something that draws out an uncool groan. "Jer, this is incredible."

She takes a hesitant bite, then shrugs as if it's nothing. "Not too bad."

"Not too bad? Now who isn't owning up to her awesomeness? You just made this up. In the winter. In the forest! How?"

"I don't know," she says through a smile. "How do you create a new world so in depth it's like I'm transported? It's what we do, right?"

She's unsettled and it's adorably modest. Before I can stop myself, I open my arm up in another invitation.

Once she's at my side, eating with a contented smile, the world seems right again.

Chapter Nine

Chase

A knock at the door breaks me away from the frosty cave where Kage is hiding out after Wilja's betrayal.

Don't leave me here you fool!

I ignore him and abandon the organized desk. Where once I'd work with papers scattered, maybe two mugs of half-drunk coffee, now my pens are in a pen holder, my notebooks are neatly stacked, and there is a chic succulent on the desk. Organized. A magazine-esque desk.

A way to maintain a bit of control over something in my life.

At the door a jolt of adrenaline grips my veins. A natural smile comes half a breath later. "Jeri! You braved the wilds of cabin life to come visit me?"

Jericho peeks out from a thick, knit scarf wrapped tightly around her face. The way her eyes gleam, I take it she's smiling under there. She pulls the scarf back, giving me a glimpse at those pink lips. "I've come as moral support."

"Moral support?"

She holds up a garment bag. "I thought you might need a shoulder to cry on when you see the final product. But the show must go on. Cookie Tinsel needs his blue elf suit or the entire festival will crumble, Chase. Just crumble. Besides, I think we established I have a thing for elves."

I forgot about the ridiculous elf suit. One positive, I suppose, is I became too engrossed in the world of the Darlings to even notice the time.

But it also means I haven't gotten dressed for the day. I take a quick inventory of my appearance, and now I wish Jericho Hunt had sent Dash or even Bruce instead of her beautiful face.

Flannel pajama bottoms, a white T-shirt with a coffee stain on the chest. My hair—I lift one hand to my head—it's on end.

Jeri steps inside, walking past me with a confidence I wish I could channel.

"By the way," she says over her shoulder. "I love the glasses. Sort of a hot, broody author look. Totally works."

Great. I snatch my black-rimmed glasses off my nose. Funny enough, even though my stomach is in a tangled knot of nerves, I smile. She likes my glasses. Huh. Heather used to tease me and call me Grandpa Paul when I wore them. I did resemble younger pictures of Grandpa, and she'd hate it if she knew I'd been self-conscious over it.

As I think of the memory, my breath catches hard and fast in my chest.

Heather. I . . . I haven't dwelled in thoughts of her for at least two days. I press a hand to my heart. The heat of guilt is there, but it's dull. Overpowered by a sense of . . . *relief*? How? After all this time, it's unsettling to feel so differently about someone who has been part of my thoughts day in and day out.

Something is changing.

My stun turns to the back of Jeri's head as she disappears into my kitchen. She is so unlike any woman I've spent time with before. A little chaotic, but in a good way. Her demeanor is thoughtful, and playful, and she yearns for creativity the same way I do. She doesn't get bored talking about different outlets. She stages a book scene in local markets, cooks me a meal inspired by laughter.

She walks into my house without an invite.

Heather supported my career, don't get me wrong, but we never really talked about work unless there was a big problem or announcement. Most days her nursing stayed at the hospital, and my writing stayed in the home office.

With such differences between them, why, then, does Jeri bring out feelings I thought were dead?

"Chase Thorn!" Jeri shouts.

It takes me a few breaths to find her. Again, inviting herself into my house and making herself comfortable has thrown me for a loop. I think I like it, though, knowing she feels comfortable. It leaves me wanting her to feel comfortable with me in different ways.

Jeri is in my kitchen, staring at the wall. Taped in four separate rows are three by five cards with different plot points, scenes, the special sauce that will hopefully make book seven of *Wicked Darlings* the book people can't put down.

"Oh, sorry," I say, embarrassed. "It's such a mess in here. Give me a second and—"

Her arm flies out, smacking me in the chest. She hasn't peeled her gaze off the wall of sloppy cards. "Don't. Touch. It."

Whoa. A surprising demanding side. It's sexy. "Uh, you're a little scary."

Jeri points a vicious grin at me. "You have no idea. Has this been what you've been doing the last two days you've ditched my perfectly lonely café booth?"

I rub the back of my neck, studying my timeline on the wall. "Yeah, I guess I got a little caught up in things after you forced me to run through the grocery store, and brainstorm Kage in the middle of the woods."

"First—the woods were totally you're idea. Second, I absolutely disagree. Running through the market was a beautiful exercise in busting down writer's block. Clearly—" She gestures at the wall. "I'm a genius."

She's so many things.

I go to her side and stare at the mess of timelines and scenes on my wall. No doubt she thinks I'm odd. Maybe it'll irritate her, the chaos of building a story. Heather would roll her eyes, and give me that 'Really?' look when this happened. Maybe that's why I keep things orderly in the writing den now.

I forgot I lost it a bit in the kitchen, though.

"I'm usually not this—" I wave my hands around my kitchen. "Everywhere."

Jeri scoffs. "Uh, you should be. This is amazing."

"Yeah?"

She reaches out and touches one of the cards tenderly. "This is incredible. I feel like I'm witnessing something wonderful unfold. You know, sort of like a chrysalis, except this is an entire world that is going to change people. It's perfect."

"Change people? I doubt that."

Jeri narrows her eyes. "You don't think your books change people? Think again, Thorn. To the guy who's so stressed out at work, you give him a few hours of escape. To the woman who's in a terrible relationship, Revna Brutus, the sassy lady pirate, empowers her to speak her truth. Words matter, Chase. Even written ones."

A rush of desire to touch this woman takes over any rational thought. I slip my fingers through hers. "Thank you."

Jeri squeezes my hand. She laughs a little nervously. "Sure. But again, this is me being selfish. Now I feel less like a manic person when I tear apart my kitchen looking for that perfect flavor."

"You can tear it apart in front of me, so long as I get to be your taste tester."

"Does that mean I get to be a beta reader?"

"Uh, no."

Jeri's mouth drops open. "Well, then forget taste testing."

I laugh and lose my mind a little more, drawing her into me, so my lips brush against her ear. A thrill surges through my blood when Jeri shudders.

"Beta readers," I whisper, "need to be objective. I don't trust you to be brutally honest."

"Take it back. This is my Kage Shade we're talking about. I will not let you ruin him."

"You think I—the creator of his entire soul—would ruin him?"

"It's been known to happen in the book world. I mean, you did play a nasty trick on him in the last book. No wonder he's stopped talking to you."

She has a point, boy.

I roll my eyes, until I realize she just acknowledged characters talk to me. This woman—she's breaking me down, and truth be told, I'm starting to love it.

I stare at our clasped hands, voice low. "He's starting to break his silence."

Jeri follows my lead and curls an arm around my waist. How long has it been since I've been touched this way? Almost like I'm wanted again. I didn't know how much I missed it until this moment.

"I'm really glad he is," Jeri says.

"I think you've had a lot to do with it."

My fingertips draw gentle circles over her shoulders. Little by little our bodies start to turn into each other. My throat goes dry as I settle one palm against her smooth cheek. Jeri's eyes drink me in; they cut me to the bone.

I rest my forehead to hers, our noses touch. Jeri closes her eyes, and gentle fingers trace the line of my jaw.

A thousand things ping pong in my head. I should say something, right? Maybe warn her that I'm rusty—no—I'm beyond rusty. I'm closed off, caged away behind barbed wire, afraid to step out of my solitude. Yet, with her, I can't seem to stay buried in the gloom.

Her thumb draws along the line of my bottom lip and I can't remember my own name.

I thought if this moment ever came it would be like tearing off a bandage. Fast and painful. But I want to move slow. I want to enjoy every second.

My fingertips memorize the curve of her neck, the soft lines of her face. My lungs fall in time with her heavy breaths and I've hardly touched her yet.

Our eyes lock for a few heartbeats. Then, I crush my mouth to hers.

All feeling abandons my body, and for a moment I'm not on solid ground. I'm floating, lost in the shock of sensation. Jeri's soft gasp. Her fingertips digging in my hair. The taste of her lips—vanilla and mint. Her curves were made for my hands.

I regain function, and a hot spark of desire takes over.

I grip her hair with a bit of frenzy, but gentle enough she smiles against my mouth when I tilt her head back even more. Her fists curl around my shirt, holding my chest, my hips, my body against hers. No space is between us, but I'm not sure I'll be able to feel close enough.

My mouth travels to her neck. I walk us to the wall, one hand on her waist, the other on her face, until her back presses against the rows of cards. She frees a soft sigh. It only spurs me to take her lips again, deep and raw.

Time whirls. It's fast and slow. We can't stop grabbing for each other. Our hands take their time, memorizing different planes of the other.

This, *this,* is something unique. Something special. I haven't felt this way before. I'd remember.

Then, like a car to the chest, guilt strikes.

I pull back, breathless. Half of one hand is lost in Jeri's hair, the other is on her waist, drawing her against me.

"I'm sorry," I say, voice rough.

"Don't be." She drags her bottom lip between her teeth.

This isn't fair. To let her believe I have a piece to give when those pieces of me are dry and brittle and gone. I shake my head and reluctantly allow my hands to drop. "No, I . . . can't do this. It isn't fair and—"

"Fair?"

"I shouldn't have done this." I grip the ends of my hair.

"Oh, my gosh." Jeri's face pales. "Are you *with someone*?"

I close my eyes against the stabbing pain in my chest, and must take too long to answer because Jeri shrieks a bit of disgust. I've never seen the woman move so fast, but in another second she's gone, cursing my name down the hallway.

What? No, she's not leaving thinking this about me. "Jeri, wait. It's not like that."

Her eyes widen. I think she's going to murder me. "You are a pig. You're just like him, famous, and rich, and think you can just *hurt* other people." I have no idea who she's talking about, but she's still ranting. "A sick, sick, sick—"

"I'm not with anyone," I blurt out. My hands go to her shoulders, and now that I've touched her again, I'm not sure I'll ever be able to stop touching her. She cuts her glare into me, and my shoulders slump. "I'm not married. I don't have a girlfriend. I promise. But I . . . I can't be with anyone else, either. It's not fair to you."

"Anyone else? Anyone else from who, Chase? What's not fair?"

"I like you," I say, trapping her face between my hands. "So much. I started liking you the second I met you. You inspire me, you make me laugh. I can't remember the last time I really laughed. You make me *feel*, Jeri."

"Then what's wrong?"

I shake my head. My voice is hardly more than a whisper. Each breath is broken and shallow. "I promised her I'd never love anyone else."

It takes a moment, but when her fingers touch my face, they're gentle. "You promised who?"

Tell her, Chase. Be a man. Explain all this and you can be friends again. Friends. It'll have to be enough. But it won't be. Even I know it.

"Heather," I croak out. "My fiancée. My *late* fiancée."

Jeri's brows lift. "She died?"

I nod, keeping my hands on her, but my eyes fall to the floor. "Almost two years ago."

She gives me a sad smile. "I'm so sorry. Do you mind if I ask how she passed?"

"Ovarian cancer," I say. They're curse words scraping over my tongue.

She squeezes my hand. "Cancer is awful. It took my grandmother too. How long were you together?"

Are we doing this? I want this woman, but she's . . . she's asking about my fiancée? I lick my dry lips and go with it. "Almost five years."

"I'm sorry, Chase. I can't imagine what that must've been like to lose someone you loved like that."

"It spread so quickly," I say before I can stop. "She was only thirty, and thirty-year-olds shouldn't die, you know? I was there when she died, and I think I said what I did because it hurt *so* bad to watch her go. I promised her I'd never forget her, Jeri. I'd never love anyone else. Never *be* with anyone else, and she opened her eyes for the first time in days and looked at me. I didn't even know she could hear me at that point, but she smiled. Like it was the peace she needed."

"Chase." She shakes her head, and holds my hand against her face. "That isn't fair to you. I didn't know her, but if she loved you like you loved her, I can't imagine she'd want you to be alone."

No. She wasn't there, she didn't see the final glance Heather gave me. So calm, so free.

But there is an undeniable passion running beneath my skin for the woman in front of me. She's not Heather, but it's okay. And I can hardly believe I think it. Jeri is different and perfect in her own way. Unknowingly, she healed a few of the scabrous, cold pieces of my heart.

My first written words since Heather passed came because Jeri cared enough to unlock them.

I close my eyes, forehead touching hers again. Her clean, soft scent stirs through my lungs. She's warm, she's weird, she's understanding. Jeri is exactly who I needed to breathe life back into my soul.

She is right about something, though. Heather did love me. We loved each other, opposite as we were. A small speck in the back of my brain believes Heather would want me to be happy, even though our happily ever after didn't work out how we planned.

Could I be satisfied knowing I loved her the best I could? Was it enough for her? Would she be happy I'd found a connection with someone else?

Am I even willing to try?

I lift my head so I can look into Jeri's eyes. For her? I think I'd be willing to do anything.

"I like you Jeri Hunt," I say again. "I can't pretend you didn't wake me up after being numb for so long."

Her chin quivers. Jeri kisses me sweetly. "Then don't pretend. I like you, too, Chase. I like you so much it scares me. I've never felt so drawn to someone else. Ever."

Should we let this slip by?

I force myself to think of anything but Heather's face. The conjured disappointment I've convinced myself she'd feel starts to fade the longer Jeri's hands are on my skin.

I want this. I'm afraid of this.

Love can end in pain. An agonizing lesson to learn.

But—I think I *want* to risk it.

"I like you, Jeri."

She chuckles. "You keep saying that. For someone with a prose as smooth as you, I'm surprised."

I smile, my arms curling around her waist. Her eyes bounce between mine. The words come slowly and with a hefty supply of caution. "I want . . . I'd like to see where this can go."

She tilts her head and strokes the side of my face. "You deserve happiness, Chase. You do. If it were different, and it had been you who died, would you want her to be alone?"

In truth, I've never flipped the tables before. No, I wouldn't want her to be alone. But I saw Heather's face, her smile, her peace in those last moments. How do I let go of something like that? Still, I'm standing here with a feeling so deep, so honest, bursting in my chest, I can't deny this holds the makings of something unique and lasting.

If only I can give it a chance.

I cup Jeri's cheek. There aren't any words I can say to make the pressure in my chest leave. It's a collision of opposites. The thrill of something new and wonderful collides with sorrow and guilt.

I kiss her.

For now, I push it all away and dive headfirst into the peace that comes from Jeri Hunt.

Chapter Ten

Jeri

Chase slams one edge of the plastic sled into the snow, so its nose is pointed at the sky. He places his hands on his hips, eyes on the slope, and poses like a man about to head into battle.

Abigail mimics his every move.

He looks at her. "Think we can handle it?"

She blows out her lips, then gathers her saucer. "I was born for this."

Chase laughs and settles over his sled, using his heels to keep him from sliding down. Abigail sits cross-legged in her saucer, a look of delight buried beneath her freckles and pink cheeks.

"Last one to the bottom owes—"

"Hot chocolate!" Abigail shrieks, then launches down the hill.

"Cheater!" A second later and Chase is flying after her. Sloan snickers and snuggles against Rowan's side. The hill behind the inn is the town's hot spot for sleds and tubes. Laughter rises over the gray clouds. A storm is coming, so today is the perfect time to take advantage of the snowless skies.

"He's funny," Sloan says after a long sip of peppermint tea in her thermos. "And definitely not hard on the eyes." Rowan clears his throat. With a grin, Sloan curls her arm around his waist. "Nothing like your mountain man chic, babe."

"She's lying, Ro," I say. "Chase is definitely easy to look at."

Rowan rolls his eyes, but smiles. "Look, I don't care if he's Man of the Year. He's good to you, and Abigail thinks he's the coolest, so I'm pretty easy to please."

"And Loo let it slip about the TV show," Sloan adds.

"Yeah, he failed to mention it when we were catching the demon magpies," Rowan says with a scoff. "I knew he wrote books, but I guess it didn't click that he was *that* big."

"Abs won't stop asking to watch it," Sloan says.

I grit my teeth and shake my head. "Uh, probably not a good idea."

"I know." Sloan takes another drink, cheeks shading a darker red. She shares a look with Rowan that looks like they're sharing a secret thought.

My brow arches. "What?"

"Nothing," Rowan says, still grinning. "What? It's nothing. Sloan might've watched the first episode."

"No, no, *husband*, don't lie! You said we needed to do intel on the guy."

"Intel? Rowan, you guys knew him as kids! And you are basically blood brothers after the magpies."

"It wasn't enough, Jer-bear," Sloan says as she pinches Rowan's arm.

"So, you figured watching his book's Netflix adaptation would fill in the gaps?" I snicker. These guys are freaks. I love them. They care like we're blood, and I'm grateful.

"It's a good way to see how a man's head works," Rowan says.

"Yeah, and tell her what happened." Sloan smirks.

"No."

"One episode, Sloan. We'll just watch one," Sloan mocks in a Rowan voice. She turns her grin on me. "Five episodes later, we force ourselves to turn it off. Do you know what it feels like to run an inn during busy season when you go to bed at two in the morning?"

"You got just as into it as I did," Rowan insists.

"Totally did. I'm borderline obsessed."

I clamp my hands over my ears. "Don't say anything else. I don't want to know. I'm waiting for season two before I watch."

Sloan looks at me like I'm insane. "Jer, you're dating the guy behind the genius and romance and gore. Ugh. I shouldn't like it so much. I mean it's *violent*, but the story."

"I know. I read the books when I first moved here, and devoured them." Something in my chest squeezes. I love that these guys like Chase. Because I like him. Oh, I like him *a lot*. "I'm just glad the last book is finally underway."

"You know you're going to be in the credits of a show, right?" Sloan folds her arms over her chest. "I mean you are the muse. You deserve top of the screen credit."

"Nah. Chase deserves the big, flashy credit for doing the work."

"Work with what?"

My stomach flutters. Chase appears behind me and presses a kiss to my cold cheek. He's breathless, and is packing both the sled and saucer on his back. Abigail flops into the snow behind him, grinning ear to ear.

"Your book," I say, following his lead and hugging his waist. "You're putting in the work."

He smiles and shrugs like it's nothing. "It's coming along."

"Rowan and Sloan were just telling me how obsessed they are with the show."

"Obsessed is a strong word," Rowan says.

"I wanna see it," Abigail whines. "Please?"

Even Chase shakes his head as he crouches at her side. "Sorry kid, I agree with your mom and dad on this one."

"Because it has the M on the rating?"

Chase nods. "M for: makes you stay awake all night because of monsters."

"The monsters are *why* I want to watch it." Abigail lets out a groan dripping in tween spirit. "And I know it means mature. I've decided mature means: *all the cool shows.*"

Chase stands, giving up the battle. "Sorry, Rowan. I'm out of comebacks."

Rowan laughs, snatches the sled, then tosses a flurry of snow on Abigail, so she shrieks. "Come on, grumpy, let's race."

My focus is lost in the buzz of the Honey Pot. The colder it gets the more people flock inside my doors looking for a bit of warmth and probably some chocolate.

Intense focus is, no doubt, the reason I nearly split my skin when Chase sneaks up to the counter, taking me by surprise. The second his hands slap the surface, I nearly splatter foamy coffee all over my sweater.

"Whoa," he says, an edible smile on his face. "Sorry. Not sure if I should be offended you didn't notice me, or if I should be impressed how you can block the world out."

I chuckle and finish with my crushed candy cane, then prop onto my toes and peck his lips. "Always be impressed."

"I am. No worries there."

There is still a shadow in Chase's eyes. He's a dream, truly, but I suspect there is a piece of the past that has a deep hook in his heart. He holds back. Not intentionally, but it's there all the same. No mistake, the man kisses me like it's his reason for breathing, his touch is fast becoming the only thing worth asking for this Christmas, and the way his eyes darken in want when he looks at me, leaves me breathless and greedy for more.

But there are times when he looks at me and . . . he wonders. Wonders if this is right, maybe? Wonders if a woman I've never met hates him? It could be all those things rolled into one, but he keeps trying, keeps stealing my heart.

Time. He's suffered the worst kind of broken heart. It will take time is all.

"Anyway," he goes on after I've successfully delivered the coffee to one of the utility office secretaries. "Have dinner with me tonight."

"Uh, always yes."

The shadow brightens and it's like a little weight lifts off my chest. See —*time*.

"Look, I know you're some fancy, famous culinary chef and all, but I'm cooking for you."

"Hmm. I like the sound of this. No one has ever cooked for me." A truth I say nonchalantly, but it gets Chase to pause.

"No one has cooked for you?"

For a few heartbeats I reel through a few past relationships. Not all pleasant. The last one rather unpleasant, truth be told.

"Nope. Can't say I've had a meal made just for me in my adult life."

Chase wears a look of determination, pointing at me. "This miscarriage of justice ends tonight, Jericho. I make a mean something. I'm not sure what it is, but I will make it."

That draws out a laugh. "Love me some mystery dinner. But why the insistence to suddenly cook for me?"

"We need to celebrate."

"Why? Oh, oh, oh, did you get them finished?" I grip his wrists over the counter, about to explode. "You've got them! The first three?"

He nods and I dance on my toes, unable to keep the thrill out of my veins.

The next thing I know my little Christmas wish of him kissing me comes true. His strong hand curls around the back of my head, and holds me for at least ten seconds. Short and sweet, but enough that some of the sheriff's deputies in the third booth let out loud whoops.

When he pulls away, the dark, addicting desire is in his eyes. "Sorry. I can't be professional right now. No one has ever made such a big deal about the little victories before. You make me feel like I've rescued a family from a burning building. I wrote three rough chapters."

His words pack a punch. In the days we've spent together—and I mean morning to night—there have been a few comments made where he hinted even Heather didn't take a huge interest in his career. From what I gather they kept their professional lives at work, and bonded over different things.

I sort of like the idea of doing both.

"We are absolutely celebrating," I say. "You can cook all you want, but I get to make you a three-chapter dessert."

"Do I get one every time I write three chapters?"

"No question."

"Noted. Sounds like I need to get a treadmill, then." He leaves me with playful smirk that twirls my insides, and returns to his booth we've now dubbed his office.

Once more, I get lost in the busyness of the café, but my heart soars. Genuine excitement for Chase's success blooms like melted chocolate through my body.

He does the same for me too. When Harold came in singing praises to my new Christmas sweet rolls, Chase insisted on buying one for every person in the café until I ran out. He said something so tasty needed to be enjoyed by everyone. Another time when I zoned out, worried about a lack of ideas, he didn't say anything. Simply stopped what he was doing, grabbed his car keys, and drove us to the market where he vividly painted a picture of a European town in the Alps.

I think I almost cried when flavors started to swirl in my head.

The bell dings and a rush of frigid air floats inside, followed by a cheery voice. Pam. My back is to the front, but her little chirps hint that she's ushering in an entire group.

"Come on, come on. Yep, in you go. Everyone have their book and pen at the ready?"

I wheel around.

What is she up to? The woman is holding the door, letting all my expensive hot air outside, and waving in at least a dozen confused-looking women.

After the last person comes in, Pam scans the Pot, then those gossip-hungry eyes land smack on Chase. He's lost in his screen, unaware he's been targeted.

"Oh, there." Pam points her long fingernail at him. "There he is."

The tone of her voice is such that I'm surprised she didn't finish up by growling, "Get him, girls!"

The hesitant women all hold a copy of the first *Wicked Darling* book. Pam whips out her phone and starts taking pictures, all while forcefully nudging the lead ladies toward Chase's booth.

"Rex Blade," Pam shouts, causing most of the café to turn and look. Chase peels off his headphones, a look of discontent on his face. Pam takes a picture, then gestures to her fan club. "These wonderful fans would love you to sign their new, exciting books. They loved the story and can't wait for more."

Oh goodness. She's filming. Literally—like she is a breaking news journalist—Pam is talking into her phone.

Chase shrinks a bit, but tries his best to smile at the motley crew. Pam loses a touch of patience and practically drags the first woman forward. It's Jenna James—Silver Creek's most timid deli worker.

Nope. This isn't going on. Not here. Not to Chase. He deserves to live here in peace.

I drop the dish towel in my hand, snap a few orders to Tayla, then march with our supplies into the dining area.

Pam is going on and on about the gloriousness of his novel. Trust me, it's snatch and grab from the back description. The woman hasn't read the book. I shove my way through, Tayla at my back.

"Jericho!" Pam lets out a little gasp when I set up our caution wet floor signs all around Chase's booth. "This is a book signing."

"No," I say, crossing my arms over my chest. "This is an ambush. Vivian?" I look to the school nurse who seems ready to melt into the ground. "Have you even read the book?"

"Uh . . ." She blinks her stare to me, then Pam, then at last to Chase. "I'm sorry, no. I'm not usually a fantasy reader, but I'm sure it's spectacular."

Chase lets out a nervous laugh and scrubs his face.

I wheel on Pam. "Pamela Tilby, you coerced a book signing?"

"Jericho, it's for our social media page. We agreed to use the intrigue of Chase's books as a way to draw out fans."

"No, we said it could be a bonus. Never that we'd attack while the man is eating lunch."

"It's already working," she argues. "Everyone is intrigued. We have folks all the way to Denver who have given a maybe on our Facebook RSVP."

"A maybe," I say with a lifted brow. "Well, by all means we should keep disturbing one of my paying customers over maybes."

Chase reclines in the bench, unbothered now. Honestly, he looks like he's enjoying the standoff. "I mean, sometimes you won't let me pay—"

"You. Hush." I point at him without looking away from Pam's feral expression. "As I said, *paying* customers."

"He's an author! Author's love book signings," Pam says in a huff.

"Do they? Do they really?" I ask. "Even if they do, you can't ambush the man."

"Jericho, you're being difficult." She gestures to the rest of the dining room. "Everyone is interested, and you're hogging him."

I have to bite the inside of my cheek to keep from laughing. This woman. "I plan to keep hogging him."

"I like where this is going," Chase adds with a wicked curl to this mouth.

If he keeps looking at me like that, then I'll need to go on break soon. For sure.

"Everyone in here is only interested because their food has been interrupted. Besides, no one cares that he's an author. They already know him. It's not news." I turn to my dining room. "New rule at the Honey Pot. We don't ambush customers even if they're famous and super hot!"

Another whoop from the deputies.

I give an agreeable nod their way and tap the top of my yellow caution sign. "This area had some flooding. It's off limits for the foreseeable time."

Pam grumbles under her breath, but slowly gathers the books from the other ladies. No doubt she bought them all. When the forced bookish crowd fades into nothing, I let out a squeak as Chase tugs my arms, dragging me onto the bench.

He pinches my chin between his fingers, his mouth inches from my lips. It's a little bit of torture the way he hovers there doing *nothing*.

"You're amazing," he whispers.

"No, I just know how to handle Pam."

"I want to be a bad boyfriend and tell you to close early so we can start our date this second."

My chest squeezes. It's the first time he's said the word boyfriend. Is that what's happening here? Man, I hope so. I run the pads of my fingers over the stubble on his chin and kiss him slowly.

"Tempting, Thorn," I whisper. "And if the afternoon slumps, you might get your wish."

He flashes those white teeth, then presses quick kisses to my lips, nose, and neck until I'm squirming against the scratch of his face.

When he finally releases me, no one is even focused on the back booth anymore.

The good thing about Silver Creek is most people defend each other. I think Chase is beginning to find his place here. People wave to him on the street. They bring him jars of hot fudge, or plates of Christmas cookies. He stopped to help Bruce with a flat tire the other day and even had Bruce talking about his plans for the holidays.

Out there, in the great big world, he can be Rex Blade. But there is a bit of relief that here, with us, with *me*, he can simply be him.

Because that guy—he's the one I'm falling headfirst in love with.

Chapter Eleven

Chase

Chili. That's my big cooking debut for Jeri.

I tried pasta. It didn't work. Next, a chicken idea, but when the recipe insisted one wrong move would cause it to go dry, I didn't risk it. But chili and cornbread—I can handle that. A staple in the winter at the Thorn house.

I scoop a bite, and my shoulders slump.

It's missing something. With a glance at my phone, I weigh my options. This'll be weird, as in I've never done it, but desperate times call for a bit of the unusual.

I *will* impress a chef with dinner. No pressure.

Swallowing a bit of pride, I do what any man needs to do when he's trying to impress a woman. I call my mom.

She answers after three rings. "Chase. Hi."

Huh, she sounds excited. My mother wasn't a bad mother at all, simply hands off in some ways. Not overly emotional. The let-you-do-you kind of mom. Our whole family was that way. We were cared for, loved, but none of us ever really dug into each other's business.

"Hey, Mom," I say, stirring the pot and squeezing the phone between my shoulder and cheek. "How are things going?"

"Oh, fine. Your Dad is never going to retire, and I'm considering a poodle."

I chuckle. "You know, I begged for a dog basically until I was eighteen. It'll be a little unfair if you get one now."

"You are thirty-five and could get your own dog. How is life in the frigid wasteland?"

I laugh at that. Mom always struggled when we came out here to visit Grandpa if the visit landed outside June or July.

"It's going well. Different than L.A., for sure."

"Understatement."

"My deep, dark secret was found out a little while ago."

"Oh." She draws it out. "And? Are mothers looking at you like you're insane for writing what you do and protecting their children? Or are the fan lines out the door?"

"Neither. Turns out small town people don't really care what you do as long as you're not a jerk neighbor."

"Well, good," she says. "I haven't heard from you for a little while. Not that we've ever been much of a call-you-up family, but I actually was thinking of you and planning to call you on Sunday. Looks like we're on the same wavelength."

"Great minds, right? I, uh, I did call for a reason." I shift on my feet. This will be weird if she asks too many details, but again—impress a chef. "I'm making your chili and I'm missing the kick you always had. It tastes like beans and tomatoes."

She pauses long enough I check to make sure I didn't lose our connection.

Then she laughs. "I think I've finally arrived as a mother. All the ladies at the gym tease about how their grown children call for food and house advice more than they ever talked to them as teenagers."

"I've officially evolved as a grownup then."

She chuckles and takes a deep breath. "I always added smoked paprika and turmeric powder to mine. And make sure you have the right amount of red pepper flakes."

I stare at my poorly stocked cupboards. Forty-five minutes—yeah, I can make it to the store and back.

"You're a life saver," I say.

"Is this an important pot of chili?"

Dumb, Chase. You've given too much away. I might not be exceptionally close with my family, but I've never been good at hiding things. It's my voice—too honest, I've been told.

"Uh, I'm . . . well, I'm cooking for someone else and I want it to be good. That's all."

Another pause. My pulse kicks it up a notch.

"Someone else as in . . . a woman?"

My hands start to sweat. Will she judge me? Be happy? Think it's too soon? I wipe my palms over my jeans. "Yeah."

What is with the pauses?

"Chase." My mom's voice is soft. "I'm . . . I think that's good, son. That's really good."

Guilt, excitement, relief, pain—it ravages my heart until it's black and blue. I've done well keeping the whispered promise buried in the back of my head while spending time with Jeri. But saying it out loud to someone else—I'm dating someone else when I said I wouldn't—it draws out a bit of guilty resentment.

I don't want to resent Heather. It's not her fault I created this turmoil, or that I made a promise I didn't know I'd come to hate. But this weird balance between honoring a commitment to a woman I loved and losing myself to a woman I'm starting to love is toying with my heart.

"You still there?" my mom asks.

I shake away the stuffy swirl of emotion. "Yeah. Hey, I need to get going and finish this up."

"Okay," my mom goes on softly. "Chase, this is okay." Curse the woman —she's perceptive. "She'd wan—"

"Hey, Mom, can I call you a little later? I think I'm burning it."

Yeah, I'm not fooling anyone. But I can't hear again how Heather would want me to move on. That moment, it was only us. Her family was there for the very end, but they didn't see her face, or her moment of peace.

"Sure," my mom says. "Good luck. I'd love to know how it goes."

"I'll give you all the dirty details. Thanks again."

I hang up before my head continues its spiral into grief and bitterness. I think of Jeri instead, creating grand scenes of her gushing over my prowess in the kitchen. Thoughts of rugged manliness lead me to think of Kage Shade.

I could add this to the book. The huntress, injured, and my burly, rough-edged assassin cooking something to keep her out of the grave. Failing to make it edible, of course. Lots of cursing, maybe a bit of comic-relief bumbling—

I don't bumble.

I grin, letting the scene play out as I return the slow cooker lid and head out the door for the last few ingredients.

Kage would absolutely bumble.

And I wouldn't be cooking for a female who tries to kill me. Learned my lesson, boy. You're botching me.

This is happening. It'll be a newer, more vulnerable side. Then again, the book has spanned a ten-year period. Kage is aging.

Aging! I'll slit you navel to nose!

Naturally he'd be softer, maybe finally ready to settle down, retire from his position as the king's assassin. Start a life with someone.

I cannot listen to this.

I settle in my car, hands on the wheel. A bit of contentment blooms in my chest. He's ready to settle down. Start a life with someone, but maybe it's not only Kage—just maybe—a piece of me is begging to try all that again too.

All those worries I had earlier fade when Jeri's glassy eyes meet mine. She flashes her white smile the second the door opens, and goes up on her toes to kiss me.

I think I'll die a happy man if this woman keeps kissing me this way.

I don't need to overthink it. At least not now. Alone, maybe, but now I want to give in to those baser emotions; I want to give in to the draw, the attraction, the heat I feel around Jericho Hunt.

I've never been a love at first sight sort of guy. If you read my books, you'd see that.

But in real life—I don't know, I can't help but think something sparked to life the second Jeri landed in my arms.

She pulls back, smiling. "I love this, but, uh, I'm freezing."

"Oh, sorry." I move aside, and drag her inside. "You're distracting."

"Likewise." She takes off her coat and drapes it over the back of a log bench in the entryway. "It smells amazing in here."

I lace my fingers with hers and lead us to the kitchen. "So, be forewarned, I realized after I offered to make dinner that I'm not a chef. I know, it's weird, I thought cooking was easy—"

She slugs my shoulder.

Laughing, I press a kiss to her knuckles and pull out a chair at the table. "I had to call my mom, Jer. So, I hope it's somewhat edible."

"Cute. You called your mom for cooking help."

"Only for you. Feel honored."

"Oh, I do." Jeri settles in the chair. "Let me have it so I can get on to thanking you for all this."

She doesn't need to tell me twice. I'm quick to dish up, but funny enough, when it's time to dig in my stomach is in knots. I'm more nervous than I was the first time my first novel was being critiqued.

Jeri laughs, spoon halfway to her mouth. "Are you going to stare at me the entire time? I don't eat glamorously."

Heat prickles in my face, but I smile. "Is this how it feels whenever you put a plate in front of someone? You need to sit and watch for their reaction?"

She laughs. "Sometimes, but not tonight. This is going to be amazing. Like I said, this is a first for me, so you could've made toast and I would've been happy."

I'm not sure I'm going to survive cooking for her again. She's a chef, for crying out loud, and here I am trying to be macho cook in—

"Ohhhh!" Jeri sort of lets out a moan that makes me want to forget dinner and kiss her instead. "Chase, this is really good."

"Don't baby me."

She give my shin a gentle kick. "I'm not. This is really good. Is that turmeric?"

"Come on, are you serious? You can really taste it?" I chuckle when she nods through another bite. Maybe she's not lying—it's not half bad.

I did burn the cornbread, though, so when we've both cleaned two bowls, there are only two squares missing from the pan of bread. We laugh as we clean up, standing close, stealing glances. Not long into it, I grab her hands and peel her away from the counter.

"I'll finish this later."

Jeri's cheeks heat in a touch of pink, and she holds tightly to my hand as I lead her out of the kitchen into my living room. These moments are where I want to stay. Soft, quiet, warm. We sit on the couch in front of my grandpa's old stone fireplace. Jeri nestles against my side and rests her head on my shoulder.

"This was really sweet of you," she whispers, her fingers stroking my face.

Jeri Hunt must have a bit of magic in her touch because it takes no time at all before my fingers tangle in her hair. My arm encircles her waist, drawing her over me on the couch.

I kiss her deep and needy. All the thoughts, the beats of my heart, have shifted. They've gone to her, and it's terrifying. It's thrilling.

I want more of it.

There is always the dark cloud of the past hanging over me like a poison I inject in myself. But Jeri is more a cure than anything.

Chapter Twelve

Jeri

"You've been spending a lot of time with Chase Thorn," Pam says as she stirs her tea.

Geez, my lips tingle simply hearing his name. I steal a quick look at the back booth. Chase has a divot in the center of his forehead, and I'm quickly learning when he stares blankly at his laptop, it's not that he's doing nothing—he's plotting. Hard.

I love it. I love looking at him. I probably could all day.

Pam snaps her fingers. "Jericho, are you listening? I don't want any funny business messing up our festival. You young people with your hot and heavy flings are the perfect recipe for broken hearts, and if—"

"Pam," I interrupt with a laugh. "You're not going to get any details from me. Now, do you want some biscotti to go? It's almost three, my friend."

Pam glances at her phone and frees a weird growl-grunt. "Fine. But we need to organize the tables for the drink stand."

"On it. We'll chat tomorrow, okay?"

Pam gives me a tight-lipped smile, but ends by saying how lovely I look today, and patting my cheek.

When the door is closed, I'm quick to the lock it, then turn a sly grin at the booth. There is no plotting going on now—at least not the bookish kind. Don't get me wrong, the way Chase is looking at me, I have no doubt he's planning something. Hopefully, the things that lead to touching and kissing and all of him close to all of me.

"So, Mr. Thorn, do you still have work to do tonight?"

"Should I? Probably. Will I? Not if you're going to come sit your butt by me. Not a chance."

I laugh and sneak into his side of the booth. His arms curl around me, pulling me into his lap. Then he buries his face in the nape of my neck, breathing deeply.

"You feel so good," he whispers.

I trace the curve of his ear, following each touch with soft kisses. "I was thinking."

"Bad idea."

I pinch his side. "Dinner here. Twenty questions. I think it's time I learn more about Chase Thorn, than Rex Blade."

He freezes, then slowly eases back, a new brightness in his eyes. "Twenty questions?"

"Yeah, you know, we ask each other a bunch of questions. I've loved goofing off and talking books and kissing—have absolutely loved that addition—but I don't know your favorite color, Chase. I need to know your favorite color or what are we even doing here?"

He laughs, kissing my neck, and squeezing me against his chest. "I'm in. There are at least a hundred things I want to ask you. And it's gray. But the silvery gray."

"See—you're unique. Who says their favorite color is gray?"

"I do."

"And I love it."

I kiss his forehead, his nose, everywhere. It's hard to stop, but there is a date to prepare for. It's out of character, honestly. There are things I don't know how to talk about, or how to explain. Fears, hurts, past mistakes. In truth, I wanted to do this to learn about him.

I sort of forgot he'd be asking questions about me too.

It's fine. I can be honest and open. He's not the same as others have been. No. Chase Thorn is different and unique. Favorite color gray—I shake my head, smiling as I walk away.

"Wait," he says. "I want to help make food. Teach me your ways."

"Oh, Chase. No one can master my ways. But I won't say no to your sexy self hanging around my kitchen."

"You want me? I'll be there anytime, Jer."

I do want him. All the time. It's intense and deep. Maybe a little scary how quickly I fell into a place where each day I want to see Chase Thorn. How quickly he took up space in my heart.

He's not a bad kitchen partner either.

Chase minces, whisks, and drizzles like a pro. There is something delightfully sweet dancing around the kitchen space with him. Whenever I try to pass him to get to the walk-in fridge, he curls an arm around my waist, and kisses me. Some slower and deeper than others. All of them send my blood racing.

When paninis and salads are made, we cuddle close together in his booth and I can't remember being as content as this before.

"Okay," he says after a few bites, "I'll start. Favorite color. It's only fair."

"Aqua."

"Not blue, but—"

"Aqua."

He grins. "Okay, aqua. Like the Christmas tree?"

In the corner is my cute, little chic tree. The topper is wrapped in pale, greenish blue ribbons, silver, and white. The rest are ornaments of snowflakes and balls in the same color scheme.

"Exactly. Okay, my turn." I scrub my hands together and give my best wicked laugh. "What does your perfect Saturday morning look like?"

Chase settles back in the booth, considering the question. "Huh, well, the scenario has changed recently. It definitely involves you, a lot to do with your lips, your body, and sitting like this." He tugs me closer. "Definitely some food—we'd need nourishment. Maybe an hour or two of Netflix. Then rinse and repeat."

"Before you ask—same," I say, kissing the top of his shoulder.

We go on like that, asking flirty, pointless questions. Least favorite job, most embarrassing high school experience, favorite books—besides Rex Blade—college love life. Chase was a little close-lipped on that one until I pinched it out of him.

"I was the literary dweeb on campus," he says. "Seriously, I lived in the library and didn't go to my first frat party until my roommate practically forced me four weeks before graduation. My love life was pretty lame." He pushes his plate away, and squares to me. "Okay, I'm curious about what made you leave California. I know you lived with your grandma, right?"

My throat tightens. I don't like talking about the move from California. *Come on, Jericho. This guy has told you things, painful things. Be a girl boss and do the same.*

"Yeah," I say, taking a long sip of water. "My dad passed in an accident when I was five so we went to live with my Nana. She helped raise me." I pause, an ache building in my chest. "I left California after some things happened almost five years ago. I never really looked back. Maybe I should've made more of an effort to go back because when my grandmother passed away, I wasn't there."

"Jer," he says, taking hold of my hand. "I'm sorry."

I wave the thought away, desperate to keep the tears from coming. "It was hard, but she was always happy for me living my own life. She told me I was bold, and like a female Paul Bunyan. I guess I wanted the complete opposite when I left California. I basically pointed at a map, picked some place in the mountains, and this has been my home ever since."

"But what made you want to leave so badly?"

My fingertips start to tingle. "Uh, it was actually a rotten breakup that made me take the plunge."

Chase lifts a brow. "Now, I'm intrigued."

"Yeah." I take another drink.

"You're nervous. Was he total tool?" A shadow passes his face. "What was his name? What did he do?"

I laugh and let my head fall to his shoulder. "I like this protective side, Mr. College Nerd."

"Hey, I might have been a late bloomer, but I wasn't a D-bag. What did Stupid do in California?"

"Already giving him insulting names?"

"Well, if he hurt you he's automatically stupid in my book." Chase grins. "In fact, I'll make him a character in my real book and kill him off."

That draws out a laugh and before I know it I'm spilling. "His name is Grady. We were together for three years. He was a film hopeful like half the population there, but he wanted to direct, not act."

"Another creative."

"Yep. Apparently I'm a sucker for them." I take hold of his hand simply because touching him soothes my nerves. "He hit a stroke of good luck with a short film. It won a Sundance award, and sort of put him on the map in indie films. Then, he was brought in on a box office movie, and his career took off."

I close my eyes, remembering how it turned sour so quickly.

"We went from best friends, creative partners, to indifferent roommates in no time. Grady started partying, and when more than one tabloid caught him—" I clear my throat. "With women who certainly weren't me, I left."

Chase stares at me, a thoughtful, somber expression on his face. "That's why you thought I was a pig when I first kissed you."

I let my shoulders slump. "Yes. You're famous, you can buy whatever you want, live however you want. For a few seconds I thought—" I wave the idea away. It's so *not* Chase, it shouldn't matter now. "Getting to know you for a few days before—well, it didn't take long to realize you're not like that. You have all those things, but you don't want the recognition."

"I'm not Hollywood famous."

"The book world is pretty huge."

He grins, a bit of color staining his face. It's that flush that gets me, though. Grady would throw a fit if someone didn't credit him. He'd buy flashy things, cars, clothes, suites, all for the recognition he craved.

Chase—he practically runs from it.

"I'm glad you realized I'm not like him," he says. "I wouldn't know how to be like him. I'm too introverted, and that sounds too exhausting, and he is absolutely stupid. To think women who want him for fame could ever be better than you." Chase shakes his head. "Tell me what movies he makes and I vow to boycott them forever."

I snicker, and rest my forehead to his. "Trust me, you'll know. According to Sloan and Rowan I make a face whenever I see one."

Chase pulls me over his lap, eyes locked on mine. I hold my breath; I don't blink. Whatever he's going to say, I don't want to miss a word. "Jeri, I want you. I might have money, but we can use that to buy Abigail more sleds, or add another room to the Pot, or start a charity, or buy more books, I don't care. It doesn't change that this—" He points between us. "Whatever is happening here means more than all that."

"Are you giving me a line, author?"

He grins. "No line. It's the truth. You've . . . you've helped me open myself again to basically the entire world. I didn't see you coming, but I'm glad you did. I'm not looking at anyone but you."

"It is a small town. Slim pickings and—"

He shuts me up by kissing me. Do I mind? Not one bit.

Chase is night and day to Grady Perkins. He's tender, attentive, humble, funny, loving. I smile when he groans as I drag my fingers through his hair. He pulls me closer, his strong hands dancing up my spine.

I fall a little harder, open a little more, and hope to dig a little deeper until I hand every piece of my heart to Chase Thorn.

Chapter Thirteen

Chase

"You're not saying it to make me happy, right?" Tasha clicks her tongue—probably at her tiny dog—in the background. "Because don't get my hopes up, then crush my heart, Chase. It's worse than asking for an extension."

"I have the three chapters," I say. Truth be told, I have five chapters and an outline for seven more.

Tasha blows out a long breath. It quivers a bit.

The woman might be constantly on the move, maybe a bit of a nag, but she cares. No doubt she enjoys her commissions off me, but I think she genuinely cares about me as a person.

"This is great," she says after a long pause. "Send them over as soon as you can."

"I will." Breath catches in my throat. A thought peels through my head, and I'm not sure if it's more surprising that I had it, or that it feels like something I simply need to do. "I'm going to put a second set of eyes on it first, then you'll have the file."

Tasha lets out a little groan. "Fine. But by tomorrow, okay? There's going to be an uprising here if people don't get proof Rex Blade is alive and working."

"A little dramatic, Tash."

"No, it's not. I saw a pitchfork yesterday. It's true."

I dare laugh. Things are always good when Tasha Lim jokes. When I hang up, my pulse beats in my head, and my palms grow sweaty. Am I going to do this? I've never asked for another set of eyes from anyone without my editor's stamp of approval.

This is like stepping into the wild. Anything could happen.

An hour later, I arrive at the Holly Berry Inn, hot drinks in hand, and a bag of cake donuts with pink sprinkles. I didn't even need to text ahead for orders. I already know preferences. Strange, how in such a short time I've come to feel at home with these people.

"Hey, Chase!" Abigail pokes her head up from behind a snow hill. Red-nosed, pink-cheeked, snow-covered. She waves and brushes a blob of snow off her knit cap. "Wanna help build the igloo?"

Two more girls pop their heads up from behind the mound, giggling.

"I one hundred percent do," I tell her. "After I go—"

"See Jeri." Abigail rolls her eyes, but a little smile is on her lips as she turns to her friends. "He's *allllwaaays* here to see Jeri."

Is this that moment? Have I officially become under attack from tween kissing noises? Let them make fun all they want. One can hope those noises become reality soon, girls. One can certainly hope.

"Hey!" I hold up the sack of hot donuts. "Are you making fun of me? No, you aren't, because if you are, then none of this for you!"

"Are those Marty's donuts?" One girl squeals. "They're like a buck each, and like, have tons of flavors."

"I know," I say. "I only buy the best. Do you, like, want some?"

Abigail and her friends fumble out of their snow drift house and sprint, slipping more than once, until they reach for the bag like dogs that've never been fed.

"My mom only gets these for birthdays," the second friend gushes over the open bag.

"Chase is loaded, though," Abigail says so nonchalantly it draws a laugh from me.

"Abs," Rowan's voice interrupts. "Uh, super impolite."

He comes around the corner of the inn carrying logs for the woodburning stove.

"Sorry." Abigail says to me, then shrugs at her dad. "You said it first."

"I did . . . *kid*," he warns, then glances at me. "I did not say that."

I adjust the drinks in one hand and take some of the wood in the other. "Gourmet donuts—the new measurement of wealth."

Rowan scoffs, and nudges the front door open with his shoulder. "To those terrors—yeah, that's all you need to get. Come on in. I think Jeri is helping Sloan in the dining room."

I go with him to the large front room, stack the logs, then follow the sound of women laughing into Holly Berry's open dining room. It's a unique inn. Old, with some of the antique charm in all the fine details. But, as I understand it, Sloan has modernized a lot of the inn. New countertops, new windows. Big game tables with marble chess boards and checkerboards near an old-fashioned stove.

The dining room always smells like the distressed wood floor is mopped in cinnamon and citrus.

My heart stutters when I see her. I want to rub the spot it aches so good, but I hurry across the room instead. Jeri and Sloan haven't even noticed us, so when I press a surprise kiss to Jeri's cheek, she wheels on me.

Once my face registers, her eyes brighten. The tight knot in my chest squeezes again. As if my heart can't help but bulge at the sight of her.

"Hey," she says, and kisses my lips. "I didn't expect to see you until tonight."

"Couldn't stay away. I come bearing gifts." I place the drinks on the table, then start handing out. "Decaf for you, Mrs. Graham. I told the girl to ease up on the nutmeg."

Sloan blows me a kiss. "You're a gem, sir. A real gem."

Burly, mountain man Rowan takes his cocoa with little gingerbread men marshmallows and a candy cane straw because everyone deserves to play an oxymoron in their own lives.

I peck Jeri's lips before I hand over the dark chocolate raspberry cocoa. She snakes her arms around my waist, neck arched so she's close, but still looking at me. "You came just in time to give your opinion on the tree festival menu. By the way, Pam wants you to have a desk displaying your books and have an unofficial book signing. And, yes, before you ask, I reminded her that Rex Blade likes blood and guts and gore. He is the anti-Santa."

I take a test-sip of my own plain hazelnut cocoa—Jeri has me hooked on the flavor at this point—and lean over the sheets of food options. "Let me guess, when you told her, she didn't care."

"Not one bit."

"Probably expects him to do it wearing that stupid elf costume," Rowan grumbles, then claps me on the shoulder. "But I bet you'll make it look awesome, man."

"Don't worry," Jeri says, patting my face. "We'll find a way out of this ambush book signing. Extreme food poisoning?"

"No. That'll look bad on you and the cafe."

"Ah, good point." She rubs her chin, and I can practically see the wheels turning. "Sudden onset of social anxiety."

"Not far from the truth."

"Oh, oh, I bet we could hire some of the local boys to play insane fans! They'll do anything for ten bucks. A feral book signing will shut it down real quick if they mess up Pam's ambiance of Christmas."

I snap my fingers. "Add on some cosplay, you know, make them dress up like characters from the show and it's a solid plan. They could attack like the king's men and the magi army and freak everyone out."

Jeri's bouncing on her toes now. "I know the Grey kids would do it. Besides they still owe me for the ice ball."

"Or . . ." Sloan interjects, holding up a hand. "Now, I know this is a wild idea, but hear me out. You could just tell Pam *no*."

Jeri gasps, clutching her neck. "Have you lost your mind? No one tells Pam Tilby no."

I take another drink, at ease. At home. "And it's way more fun brainstorming ways I can take the focus off the fact that I'll be wearing tights."

"Hose. And trust me, you in skintight pants—" Jeri lets out a little moan. "I will be inappropriately staring at your lower half. All. Night. Long."

We fall into a comfortable conversation. I give a thumbs up on the festival menu. Rowan and Sloan go over a few updates they plan to make in one of the bedrooms, Jeri tells a funny story of a debate between a few deputies and some of the firemen this morning. Apparently they pulled a scene straight out of *The Office* TV show and had a heated, misogynistic battle over a certain actress being hot or not.

"All I'm saying is Ralph and Dustin shouldn't debate when they're armed," Jeri says.

For a moment I'm a silent participant watching the back and forth between the friends. In two weeks I've gone from broody, antisocial, uninspired author to a guy who knows hot chocolate and donut preferences for other people.

I steal a look at Jeri over the rim of my cup. The way she arches her throat when she laughs is addicting. She's made of soft curves, of brightness, of everything I thought I'd never have again. From the mischief in her eyes, the passion in her food, the tenderness of her touch, I'm lost to her.

Guilt is still there.

I know I'm avoiding it, but it's such a sour thought that hangs around like an ugly growth in the back of my head. I don't want to spoil this new peace I've found with Jericho Hunt.

More than past promises, though, another snag in my perfect contentment keeps smacking me upside the head.

Living here—it was never supposed to be permanent.

My life is in Los Angeles. Jeri's is here. I know the pressure will come to return. It's simpler. My publisher is there, my agent, my lonely apartment. Deadlines are fast approaching, and my life will be caught up in the whirlwind of publishing, traveling, signings, and interviews soon enough.

Jeri is established in Silver Creek, and as busy as me.

Would she want to be swept away on the ride?

A problem to stew over later, like tomorrow, or next week. Yes, next week is a better time to think of all that. Tonight, I have a question I need to ask, and no mistake, I'm a little terrified.

Later, when we're alone, I lace my fingers with Jeri's as we walk to her place in the guest house buried in the trees behind the inn. Her house isn't huge, but it's cozy. Old in some ways like Holly Berry, but she has a stone fireplace that makes it feel like I've walked into a Christmas card.

"Jer," I say, tugging on her hand, so she smashes against my chest. "I need to ask you something."

"What's up?" A groove forms between her brows. "You're nervous. Is something wrong?"

"No. Nothing wrong, but I'm a big wimp about this kind of stuff. I need to send in the chapters to my agent, but I was . . . I was wondering if you'd read them first."

"Really? You said you didn't want beta readers who might not be objective."

"To me this is more than a beta read," I admit. "I think of it more like someone who cares about me—" I pause, testing what I've said. Jeri looks at me as if that should've always been obvious and gives a little nod for me to go on. "Someone who cares about me, and knows the characters, who might be willing to give honest feedback. Someone whose ideas inspire me."

She gives me a pinched smile, eyes glistening. Before she says a word, Jeri kisses me, the taste of her knocking the wind out of my lungs.

I would've asked her this days ago if I knew this was the reaction.

She pulls back too soon—much too soon—and curls her fingers around my shirt. "I would love to read them. More like be honored to."

"Okay." I let out a nervous breath. "But you have to promise me you'll be honest."

"I promise. This really unsettles you doesn't it? All your success and having me read three chapters has you all twitchy."

"I've never done this before. My beta team is set up through my publisher. I don't see their faces when they read." I reach for my cell. She'll need to read them on my screen. Not ideal, but I formatted them well enough, I think, to make it more readable.

She takes it from me, a shadow over her face. "You never shared them with Heather?"

I brace for the smash of gloom. Of the bitter reminder that I'm betraying a dead woman. But . . . it doesn't come. I simply respond. My mind doesn't even take a detour. "We didn't do the whole work talk thing. And Heath was no fantasy fan."

"Got it. Well, as you know, I practically inhale fantasy. So, let's do this."

We just had a normal conversation about Heather. A back and forth without awkward pauses. Without grimaces. Without pain.

A little scoff comes from the couch. Jeri winks at me, pointing at the screen.

"I already like the opening. Perfect for how the last book ended and so *him*." Jeri starts to read aloud, her grin spreading with each line. *"Kage was in a foul mood. Not surprising. He was rather foul, even for an assassin. But tonight he planned to take his disposition out on others. His first target —a drunken nightwatchmen who refused to cease singing in his cups. One more word and by a count of three, make no mistake, the fool would lose his left ear."*

I drum my fingers against my legs as she chuckles again, then turns back to the screen, thumbnail between her teeth, one knee hugged against her chest.

With a bit of caution, I sit beside her, and lean on my elbows over my knees.

Every sound she makes, a hum, a snicker, a click of the tongue, draws my attention. I don't say anything, don't look at her expressions. It's a strange kind of torture.

No matter the level of success a person reaches, there are some things that will always draw out the imposter in the mind that tells them they aren't good enough.

Do I write well? Clearly, I have some loyal fans. But there is something painfully vulnerable having a woman who holds so much of my heart read the first words I've put to pages in nearly two years.

By the time I'm ready to pull out my hair waiting for the end, Jeri rests my cell on her lap, and follows it with a sigh.

The moment of truth.

I tilt my head, hair a mess because I have been gripping the ends, and wait.

Then wait some more while she stares at the wall with a smile. Two more breaths, and I break. "You need to tell me what you think, or my bones will melt."

"Vivid," she says. Jeri scoots an inch closer and props her chin on my shoulder. "Chase Thorn—I think it's safe to say, Rex Blade is back."

The breath spills out of my throat. Rips out is closer to the truth. It stings, but it's rife in relief. "You mean that?"

She nods and plays with the curve of my ear. "I loved these. I hate you a little, but only because I'll need to wait for more. It's truly such a good start."

"Any, uh, any thoughts or changes?"

Jeri crosses her legs beneath her, and squares her shoulders to me. "Just a few, nothing huge, but I have some thoughts. Take the feedback how you will."

She pulls the pages back up on the screen, and my heart swells as she digs into the chapters. Feedback, ideas, thoughts as a reader on how the characters could yank at her heart a touch more. She mentions a thought about an interaction between a woman and Kage. I laugh as she describes an image of the middle-aged, foul-mouthed woman getting the better of a trained assassin, then tossing him out on his backside.

It's right in line with scenes I've conjured myself. Time to look a little deeper into the ideas, and I think it will be perfect after the gut wrenching ending of the last book to start on a lighter note.

"I'm guessing this huntress woman is the new love interest," she says, snuggling against my shoulder.

I lift a brow, and motion zipping my lips.

Jeri traps my face between her hands. "Talk! I have ways of making you."

"Please do." I lie back, and pull her over me, holding her chest to chest. My mouth hovers close to hers. "Thank you. This meant a lot to me."

"*You* mean a lot to me, Chase."

Oh, the things I want to tell her. How she freed something inside of me when I thought it was long dead. Her laughter. Her kindness. Her eccentric ideas. All of it is knotted in the center of my chest.

I don't always speak words well. I suppose that's why I write them. Instead of butchering the truth, I kiss her. I kiss her until she understands everything.

Chapter Fourteen

Jeri

"I need to be honest," I say, pressing a kiss to his knuckles as we walk. "I think it's sort of sweet how nervous you get whenever you're going to talk about your books. You've achieved author stardom, and you act like this is your first rodeo."

Chase lets out another heavy breath and tugs at the cuffs of his suit coat. "I do get nervous and I don't know why. I think we all have a degree of confidence in our work, right? But there is also a bit of discomfort too. Not to mention, teenagers are usually the worst audience. They stare at you like you're this old, outdated thing who doesn't know what they're talking about."

"Have some experience, do you?"

He doesn't really answer, but his mouth tightens, eyes locked on the building, then he shifts a little more on his feet.

I could devour him. Not in a weird way, but all of him warms all of me. He's modest, humble, a little uncertain about his own awesomeness, and I love it about him.

I love him.

Gah! I love Chase Thorn so much.

And I have no idea how to tell him.

He looks ridiculously handsome right now to make matters worse. I've never seen him in a suit. No tie, with the top two buttons undone. He's going to be the death of me any second. The scruff, the styled hair. Frankly, this little visit needs to hurry up so we can move on to more private moments.

I try to forget that I've only got Tayla covering the Pot for two hours. *But* after the café closes, this guy is all mine.

"Ready?" I ask.

He nods, takes my hand like it's his way to breathe, then opens the door to the high school.

Inside, the hallway blasts us with a heady hint of overused heaters and teenage attitude. A few wandering kids pass us, never lifting their eyes from their phones, but I think Chase prefers it this way. Quiet, alone, no gawking eyes.

He starts to relax and my fingers can breathe again.

We wander into the office. It's quiet, but Bea, the old secretary notices us and smiles. "Hi, Jeri. And hello to the famous Mr. Blade. Pam has called at least half a dozen times to make sure we roll out the red carpet. I'm not sure what she expects us to do, but there is the teachers' lounge with three vending machines instead of the one in the common area."

I snort a laugh and hold tight to Chase's arm. "I think Chase prefers under the radar, so no worries, Bea."

"True," he says, voice rough.

Bea snickers. "Well, I don't blame you. By the way, William certainly appreciated the help with that jack the other day, Chase. I wanted to let you know in case his grumbly grunts were lost in translation."

Chase finally smiles. "Paul Thorn was my grandpa, Bea. I know how to speak stubborn man."

Does my heart skip a beat knowing Chase is *that* neighbor? Yes. It does.

Bea and her husband William live two cabins away from him, and don't have a lot of young, strong help as William says since their two boys moved to different states.

"Well, even still, I brought you this." Bea hums as she digs into the desk drawer and pulls out six blocks of homemade fudge. All different flavors.

"Bea, next time call me to fix a car if it means your fudge," I tell her. It's not meant for flattery. The woman has a gift and will have her own booth at the festival. I've tried to get her to sell some at the Honey Pot all year, but she insists she doesn't have the time.

As Chase accepts his haul, the door to the principal's office swings open. Pace Hewitt went to school with Rowan and Sloan, and since I'm friends with the Graham's, to Pace, it means I've been grandfathered in as a local who's lived here her whole life.

He's at least six foot five, and buries me when he slings a long arm around my shoulder.

"Jericho. Chase. Thanks for coming. The kids'll love it. I should warn you, though, there've been a few rumors of some senior girls who are extra happy you're a single famous dude. You catch what I'm saying?"

"Tell them I'm not interested in jailtime, and I'm not single," Chase says in a hurried breath.

I lock my fingers with him, needing to touch him. It's not enough. Not even close.

"No worries, man," Pace says, gripping Chase's shoulder, his expression entirely serious. "We'll call out the guard. They won't get close to ya. Oh, by the way, Shan wants you two to come over for Sunday dinner sometime. We'll get Rowan and Sloan, maybe take out the snowmobiles, and have a day of it."

Ah, small towns.

One minute you're talking like acquaintances, the next you're getting Sunday dinner invites.

I'm not sure if it's Chase's sort of thing, but he smiles and nods. "Sounds like a plan."

He fits here. I remember what it was like to be a transplant from an entirely different world than Silver Creek. Chase has adjusted better than me. Maybe it's because he spent time here as a kid, but I've come to love this town, so it matters that he's finding his place too.

Pace claps his hands and gestures for the door. "Should we get this over with? The kids already love you, man. You got them out of class for an assembly."

Maybe Pace knows how to read people better than I thought, because he keeps Chase distracted all the way to the auditorium, then has him on the stage in another twenty seconds, ready for this school visit Pam set up without giving him much warning.

"It'll really draw out the younger crowd to the festival if they know his success story, and see his handsome face before their break," she told me yesterday.

I quickly learned Chase is a sucker for kids, and was sold when she tried to spin this as a teaching, inspirational moment that will help them reach their potential.

Pace agreed with Pam and told him to try to make this into a motivational speech for the kids. A shoot for their big goals kind of talk.

From the wings of the stage, I watch him fall into the story of his road to Rex Blade. I think he nails it. He doesn't have the rags to riches story, or anything, but he talks about self-doubt. About rejection, then turning rejection into motivation. He tells them about the importance of work, the action steps needed to get to the place they want to be.

At the end, there is time for a Q & A. Two microphones are placed at the front where kids can line up. This was the part that Chase worried about, that no one would come or care enough to talk.

"It's the crickets in a conversation thing," he said. "You sit there waiting, and no one ever asks anything, or cares to know more."

I can laugh about it now because the second Pace gives the go ahead, students pounce for their chance to ask Rex Blade a question.

I've got to hand it to Silver Creek High, most of the questions are thoughtful. They're earnest. Even rough and tough freshman Tyler Long stands up and asks, "What if you write books in verse?"

Chase's expression changes to a bright sort of thrill. "That's a solid writing style, and not easy. Do you write in verse?"

Tyler glances around the room, unsettled, then gives a little nod.

"Talk to me after," Chase says. "I'd love to see some."

"Really?"

"Absolutely. I've always admired verse storytellers."

This man—he doesn't even realize how captivated he has a bunch of hormonal people. If they're not interested in writing, they're interested in his fame, but if they are interested in writing, they're getting advice.

A few guys ask what's the most expensive thing he's ever purchased.

"L.A. rent," he says, drawing a few laughs.

Lake, a tall girl with a puffy ponytail, steps up. Pace gives a little gesture from the wing, with a knowing nod. I think I follow. She must be one of Chase's fangirls. Her dad is the fire lieutenant. And if I know Grant Pierce —and I do because I feel like I know everyone—he would not be on board with his seventeen-year-old fangirling over a full-grown man.

He's the epitome of the pro in protective dad.

"So, two questions," Lake says. "Are you . . . are you single, and what's the youngest you'd ever—"

Pace clears his throat in the microphone, shaking his head. "Miss Pierce."

"It's not just me who's wondering, Mr. Hewitt."

I cover my mouth to keep from laughing. Poor girl—she's the unlucky one who got picked to be the spokesgirl.

"He's with Miss Jeri at the Pot!" a boy somewhere in the dark auditorium shouts.

More oohs and ahhs and whistles follow. My stomach falls out through my shoes, and Chase rubs the back of his neck. At least he's smiling.

"Well, there you have it," he says into the mic. "Does that satisfy the question?"

Lake nods and hurries away amidst a few bawdy cheers from kids in the crowd.

"On that note," Pace says. "We're going to stop."

There are groans in the audience, and I'm not sure they could've offered a sweeter sound to Chase Thorn. The kids who didn't get their questions answered look dejected, so Chase leans over and whispers something to Pace.

The principal smiles and nods. "Hey, anyone who didn't get a chance to ask an *appropriate* question, Mr. Thorn has graciously offered his personal email, so you can send them. Do not abuse it."

The kids disperse with their teachers. Pace shakes Chase's hand and reiterates the invite for a future Sunday dinner, then at last, it's only us for a quiet moment.

I hug him from behind, and press a kiss between his shoulder blades. "That was perfect."

"It went a lot better than I thought. The last school they put me at was a middle school. A *middle school* to talk about my adult fantasy books. No one but a few teachers had read a page. For good reason, obviously." He faces me, drawing the line of my jaw. "Sorry you got called out."

"I'm not." My arms tighten around his waist. "Now all the teenagers will leave you alone. They're scared I won't give them free hot chocolate samples if they cross me."

Chase kisses the tip of my nose. "Thanks for being here, but we better get to work."

"We?"

"Are you kidding? You holding my hand while I'm a big, nervous baby means I'm working for you the rest of the afternoon. I've been learning the process, no worries. I can make a killer cup of coffee at this point."

He takes my hand and pulls me out of the auditorium. Halfway down the hall, Tyler finds us and Chase gives him a different email from the Rex Blade address. His real personal email.

"Thanks Mr. Thorn, I sort of thought I was weird for writing that way, but it's just how the words come."

"Then that's how you write them," he says. "Looking forward to reading some of it. You're good with criticism?"

Tyler nods. "I have an older sister who thinks she's a literary professor since she's majoring in English Lit. She's torn them apart. I'm pretty used to it at this point."

"Then you're already miles ahead of where I was at your age. Looking forward to it."

Tyler flushes a little, but waves before he rushes off to the last few classes of the day.

Outside, a harsh wind starts to blow, drifting flurries of snow at our faces. I snuggle closer, tugging the collar of my coat around my chin. Chase slips his fingers into mine, and pulls me through the parking lot. This close to lunch, there are a few students leaving the campus for food. Doubtless half will show up at the Honey Pot in five minutes. Some girls stare at Chase with a wistful kind of glance. The boys give me a thumbs up.

"Way to hit it big, Miss Jeri!"

"Markus! Don't cross a line or no more mocha whipped cream!" I shout at the burly football player. A hometown hero of a kid for carrying Silver Creek High to a State Championship victory. He's a brat and never stops joking. But he's a cute bratty jokester.

Markus holds up his hands and opens the door of his mom's suburban for one of the girls. "Hey, I just say it like it is, Miss Jeri. S'not like Mr. Thorn isn't leveling up, cuz he is."

"That's more like it, kid!"

"So, all the whipped cream?"

"For now."

When the kids leave us in peace, Chase nudges my back against the freezing metal of his car. His cold palms frame my face, drawing heat that shouldn't be there. His eyes hold mine for five breaths, as if he wants to memorize my face and this moment.

"He wasn't wrong, Jer." His mouth teases my cheek. "I leveled up."

"Ah, you only think that because I haven't shown you abnormal Jeri, yet."

"Abnormal Jeri? So playing out a fantasy battle in a supermarket is normal Jeri?"

"Absolutely. I'm surprised you've never done it before now."

He smiles, then dips his head, kissing me like a boy about to take his girl behind the bleachers. A tad indecent for high school, but look how much I don't care.

It's as if Chase awakens something inside me. His touch breaks me and stitches me back up in the same breath. His ideas inspire me on a level I've never reached before. I've been alone for a long time; I don't think I realized until he filled a piece of me that had been on empty all this time. I have my friends, but Chase, he's taken command over a different piece of my heart.

So, those reasons—those are why I don't care if the man takes his time with a kiss. If he adds a touch of passion that might make teenagers blush.

In fact, I don't care if every snoopy busybody in this town sees us.

Me falling head over heels for the new guy in town? Well, this is one rumor I don't mind being spread.

Chapter Fifteen

Chase

The phone is dark and taunting. *Come on, Tasha.*

I've been waiting for any sort of response from my agent. She's had the revised chapters with a few additions from Jeri's feedback for twenty-four hours. If there were ever someone who didn't hold back on feedback it's Tasha.

I'm supposed to finish my latest chapter, then meet Jeri at the old Main Street square where the tree festival will revolve around the enormous pine tree. Pam continues to insist we're partners on the festival committee, but the truth is Jeri and I have led the charge. From drinks to napkins, we've organized and arranged it all. Pam, Dash, Bruce, and the others have all been aloof overseers, only jumping in when they feel the urge to micromanage.

I can't really complain.

The lack of help from the others has given me plenty of one-on-one time with Jericho Hunt.

One of my very favorite things by now.

I wind up for my second lap around my kitchen when my phone buzzes. My fingers tremble with nerves as I snatch the phone off the table. "Tash."

"Chase," she says slowly. Is this good? Bad? Does she hate the new voice I've given Kage? She can't hate it because it feels so perfect for him now, and if she hates it I'll be at a loss on who my assassin has become.

"Well?"

She lets out a long breath, but when she speaks a smile lives in her voice. "These are amazing, Chase. Truly. It's different in feel and tone, but I think it's exactly what the book needs for the last installment. I even sent it to the editors a smidge early, and Gretchen wants more. In fact, she said she's going to email you and harass you until you get them done. Where is this coming from?"

I lean against the wall, rubbing the ache free of my head. "I don't know. I guess I needed the mountain air."

I needed Jeri Hunt.

"Well, whatever it is, I'm breathing again. I took the liberty to secure the meeting with the studio. The reps will be here at the agency on the twentieth at three. Expect a few meetings, you know, just like last time."

I nod even if she can't see me. The negotiations and planning took two weeks when the adaptation was picked up. Since I'm considered a consultant, I was in a lot of them. Tasha and the publisher's PR team more so, but they were exciting, sometimes boring, and I'm not sure I'm ready to do it all over again. Yet, at the same time, I can't wait.

"I shouldn't say this so prematurely," Tasha tells me, "but they are dropping big hints that they're looking for a contract adjustment for an additional two seasons!"

I'm a writer. I live for it; it's all I've ever wanted to do. But to see the words from my head blow up in such a way—I can't describe it.

"Really?"

"Really, Chase. Really. I knew you could do this. I never lost faith in you, my friend."

"Thanks."

"Okay, see you in the city on the twentieth right?"

"I'll be there."

We hang up and I take a few seconds to absorb it all. My agent is happy. Book sales are on the rise, so my publisher is happy. Ratings are enough to discuss multiple seasons.

All of it compounds into one truth—the only person I even care to tell is Jeri.

Timing couldn't be better. The moment I pull up to the café, Jeri turns the open sign to off and pulls a shade.

I shut off the car, smiling, and hurry to the door before she switches the lock. She startles when I smack a palm to the glass door, but it stirs my heart a bit when she beams like I might be the best thing she's seen all day.

"Hey, you," she says, going up on her toes to kiss me. "I was just about to head out and stalk a hot author who lives in the woods. Wanna come?"

"Yes," I say, stepping into the cinnamon and spice heat of the Honey Pot. "You're pretty hot, too, I bet he'll invite you inside."

She wiggles her eyebrows. "One can hope. So, what's up? You're smiling weird."

"This is just how I smile, Jer."

"Nope." She touches the corner of my mouth, kissing me there a second after. "This is the smirky, something's up smile. Your happy smile squints your eyes. And your sexy smile looks like you've got a secret you're not going to tell anyone."

Each word sort of pummels my chest. In so short a time she's learned all these details. The more interesting part is that I've learned the same about her. When Jeri is pensive she sighs every few breaths, almost as if the sound helps her think. Or when she's excited, she bounces on her toes and squeezes her fists like she's keeping in an explosion just under her skin. I know when Jeri looks at me with a half-smile, she's thinking whether or not she should say what's on her mind. When she laughs, really laughs, her head falls back and her eyes close.

It's the best sound in the world.

"So," she goes on, lacing her fingers with mine. "What's up?"

"My agent called." I pause. Everyone pauses on me, it's my turn to add a bit of dramatic effect.

Jeri rolls her eyes, squeezing my hand. "Annnnnd?"

"She's obsessed."

The toe bounce happens almost immediately. She lets out a little squeal and wraps her arms around my neck. When Jeri pulls back, her face is flushed with genuine excitement. I freaking love this woman.

"So, what's next? Studio talk? My second season?"

I laugh. "Yes. And I don't want to get too ahead of myself, but Tasha hinted these next meetings are going to be talking multiple seasons."

"Chase," Jeri says, her palms on my face. "Congratulations. This is so exciting."

"We start on the twentieth and they can take a little while. So, I'm hoping you might want to come stay with me in L.A., we could go see your cousins, and I could even introduce you to the parents if you dare."

"The twentieth? That's sort of close to the festival."

I scratch the back of my neck, embarrassed that in all my excitement I forgot about the festival. "Yeah, it might mean we need to make an awkward call to Pam."

Jeri hesitates. It cracks at my chest knowing I've put her in an internal battle. She's worked hard on this festival, probably has every year long before I showed up. Now, I'm whisking her away to the city to follow me around while I sit in boring meetings that tell me how I'm not writing fast enough, then in the next breath how amazing I am. It's a back and forth, but the thought of going at it alone is worse.

"And they wouldn't be able to move them until after the holidays?" she asks with a cautious smile.

What's going on in her head? I don't want to pressure her to be with me, and I don't think her nerves are coming because it's a getaway with me, it's just something is there.

"I wish," I say. "Two producers and the head marketer at my publisher will be out of town for three weeks after Christmas. This is really the only time we can meet before preproduction would need to start."

She nods, that same cautious smile on her face as she wipes already clean tables. "Okay."

"Jer, I don't want to make you feel like you have to—"

"No," she says quickly. My shoulders relax a little when she pecks my lips. "No. This is . . . this is important. It's amazing. I want to come. Pam will need to accept that sometimes life happens, right?"

I brush a lock of her hair off her face. "Think it'll take Pam five, or ten years to forgive us?"

Jeri snorts. "You have a prettier face, so you're looking at three years tops. Me, I'll be in Pam jail until I turn fifty, and only because she'll insist on throwing me one of her half-century parties."

I kiss her, trapping her face between my palms. "Thank you," I whisper against her mouth. "Thank you for doing this."

She smiles. It's guarded. She's holding in thoughts, and I make grand plans to get them out of her before this trip is over.

Chapter Sixteen

Jeri

I'm not sure I'll even get a half-century party.

I glance at my phone at the latest Pam Tilby update.

Sloan: She's currently trying to convince Dash to buy you out at the Honey Pot.

Rowan: I don't think she understands how real estate works. You can't just declare you're buying a commercial business.

Sloan: I DECLARE I'm buying this café! *gif of The Office bankruptcy episode*

I swallow the scratch in my throat, wishing I could be as lighthearted about it. At least through text, they don't see my face and I can hide the disquiet.

Me: *laughing emoji* I bet she'll head to Crimson to have her hack into my security system next. Probably convince me I'm under attack or there is a ghost in the Pot.

Sloan: I might encourage that one actually. Oh, maybe we could have Crimsy do something at the Inn over Halloween. Murder Mystery dinners are getting popular and she could make it extra creepy.

Chase laces his fingers with mine as all around us people fill the narrow plane aisle. "Ready?"

I give him my best I'm-perfectly-not-nervous smile and shoot off the last text. **Hey, we landed. Good luck with Pam. Don't let her commit arson or anything.**

Rowan: We've got your back. Abs will want to serve as security guard.

Sloan: She'd be the sneakiest.

Me: Love you guys! Put Abs on the case. Seriously.

Sloan: Good luck, and tell Chase good luck.

Rowan: Already texted him. What, you didn't, babe?

Sloan: *eye roll emoji* Not all of us have a weird bromance with Chase.

Me: I like my bromance with Chase. I really like it.

Rowan: Mine is deeper, Jer. You can't fight a love like ours.

Sloan: Uh oh, jokester Rowan is coming out to play for the once a year sighting.

I snicker and grab my carry-on bag. **I'm going now. Keep you updated.**

The worst part of flying is getting off the plane. Prove me wrong.

We're shuffled, smashed, squeezed, until all of us impatiently disembark into the terminal.

"So, what's first?" I ask once we're outside waiting for a car.

Chase drapes an arm around my shoulders, and rubs my arms to fight the slight California chill. To the locals it's probably freezing, to me who's lived for years in the Colorado mountains, it raises a few goosebumps.

"Drop our stuff at my apartment," Chase says, "and if you're not terrified of the idea, my parents want to meet us for dinner."

Heat fills my face. Meet the parents. It's a clear step in any relationship, and I want to take it, yet my stomach is dipping like I'm on a rollercoaster. It's been too long since I've done the whole relationship thing.

What if the Thorns hate me? I'm a small town chef with bills and an income that narrowly pays them with a tad extra for fun. What if they think

I'm only dating Chase because of his success?

People think that sometimes, right?

Especially women who date successful men. I'll need to pass an added layer of scrutiny test.

"Jer," his gentle voice calms the nervous wave as he draws his mouth next to my ear. His breath on my neck sends a delightful shiver down my back. "My parents don't pry. I swear they'll ask surface questions, and won't grill you."

"I'm good," I hurry to say. "This is just pretty new between us so I don't want them getting the wrong idea about me."

"Wrong idea?"

"That I'm after this." I swat the bulge in his back pocket where his wallet is.

He chuckles and kisses my temple. "They won't. I've talked down my income so much over the years, I'm pretty sure they think I'm on the verge of homelessness."

He's joking, but it works. It's his magic trick I love about him. Somehow he can touch me, hold me, and worries disappear.

At least for a little while.

The drive to his apartment takes nearly two hours, and I'm promptly reminded of another reason I wanted to move to a small mountain town. Traffic.

Chase's apartment is nice. An upper floor one-bedroom with a large window that overlooks the city. His kitchen is huge for an apartment, and it's the first thing I notice.

I trail my fingers along the stone countertop, touch a few copper pots. Inspect the gas stove. "Maybe we—"

"No," he interrupts. The man doesn't even lift his eyes off the stack of mail he gathered from the P.O. box downstairs.

"You don't know what I was going to say."

"You're not cooking." Chase raises a sly brow. "You, Miss Hunt, are to kick up your feet and relax for a little while."

A second later those arms are around my waist, holding me against his body.

"Maybe, Mr. Thorn, I want to impress your parents and woo them with my cooking so they'll like me."

He kisses the tip of my nose. "Maybe you'll have to trust me that they'll love you without tasting your food—which would absolutely make them love you—but so will just Jeri. Just you."

There he goes again. I'm a butter sculpture in his hands. And yes, I know how to sculpt butter, so I know when I'm malleable and melty. The next few hours turn from the Silver Creek slow pace to a bit of a cyclone. I'm not sure if the ground shifted, or a spark of electricity ran through the city when we landed, but soon enough Chase is getting calls from his agent, his editors, video chats with a few people at the publishing house, and I'm given permission to snoop through his apartment while I wait.

It's not terribly enormous, so my snooping ends in his bedroom. On his dresser, I admire an antique wristwatch collection, some old notes about *Wicked Darlings*, but stop at a photograph tucked underneath the box of watches.

An old wedding announcement that looks like it's been untouched for years.

My heart stills in my chest.

He looks happy, so does she.

Heather was beautiful. Sassy, short hair. A bright smile. Stiletto fingernails. She looks at Chase in the picture like I look at him now.

"You really loved him. Girl, I totally get it." I smile at the picture. "He loved you too. I think he's finding a way to be happy, though, and I think that would make you happy, right?"

A weird, warm connection forms to a woman I've never met. A woman who isn't here to look at the guy she loved anymore.

Tears burn behind my eyes, the hair on my arms raises. Maybe I'm talking myself into it, but there is a fleeting moment that leaves me thinking she's aware of me, and maybe she doesn't want to haunt me for loving her man. More like she's on board with it.

I hope so.

Weird, wanting the approval of a dead woman.

"I've got his back," I whisper at the image of Heather's laughing face. "I'll love him like crazy. Promise."

Geez. Now I'm making promises. She's an easy person to vow to, and I've never met her.

"Jer?" Chase calls from the hallway. He pokes his head in the room, and I let the picture fall from my hands. In one hand he holds the thin pea coat I brought, and with the other he adjusts his jacket over his shoulders. "You ready to go?"

I nod, hoping he didn't see me talking to the picture of his dead fiancée.

Should've known the man is perceptive.

His eyes flick to the top of the dresser where a corner of the old announcement is poking out from behind the watch box. His smile fades a bit as he comes over, and picks up the announcement. "I forgot I still had this."

"She's beautiful."

Chase glances at me. "Jer, are you crying?"

Oh, my—I whip my fingers to my face. Sure enough my cheeks are wet. There's nothing to do but laugh. "We had a chat, and it got emotional."

Chase tilts his head, confused.

"Don't look at me like that," I say, accepting my coat. "I let her know I'm looking after you, okay? Didn't know I was going to be a bawl baby about it."

Chase studies me like it's the first time he's seeing me. The walls sort of feel like they're crushing in on me.

He thinks I've lost my mind. We should go. Eat. Ignore the fact that I'll probably embarrass him with his affluent parents because I say something snarky about their super famous, super hot son who could have anyone he wants in the world and—

My rambling stops when Chase pulls on my arm, smashing me against his chest. A gasp sneaks out of my throat. His fingers tangle in my hair, arching my face to his.

"I love you, Jeri."

Butter legs take hold, fierce and without warning. Without his arm around my waist, I think I'd be a crumbled mess at his feet. My fingertips touch the stubble on his chin, reveling in the heat of his skin, the pulse in his neck.

"I love you too."

When he kisses me again, I don't think of anything else except that this is exactly where I want to be. In his arms, in his heart.

It's where I always want to be.

Chase's parents are perfectly polite. I don't know what I was worried about. In my head I imagined Mama Thorn charging me in defense of her boy's honor and livelihood. At the very least, I expected a bit of an interrogation.

But we've chatted, they've asked about my café, my life in Colorado, my family. Chase made a lot of promises of my special coffee if they come visit.

It sends my heart spinning in the good ways.

I tangle my fingers with his underneath the table.

"Will you two be here over Christmas?" his mom asks. She has the best name—Rose Thorn. I mean, I feel like she might've fallen in love with Chase's dad, aka Brian Thorn, partly to claim such a name.

Chase looks at me. "I don't know. Guess it depends on how many meetings we need to have while we're here."

Brian scoffs and takes a drink. "They had you running wild during the first negotiations. Stakes are even higher now. Can't imagine they'll ever let you leave the office with all that's on the table now."

I keep a steady grin, but there is a heaviness in my gut.

A flashback to all the chaos this city can bring. Negotiations, lucrative deals, fame, fortune—all the things that can get in the way of a calm, peaceful life.

This is Chase. He's not like that. He hates the spotlight. He loves me, and I come with a small, quiet town full of nosy neighbors and hazelnut coffee. I draw a deep breath through my nose and tighten my grip on his hand.

We're good.

"It'll be busy," Chase agrees. "But at the same time, we have a full season under the belt, six books, a solid fanbase. Who knows, it might go a lot easier now that we know what we're doing."

See. We're absolutely fine.

I lean a little closer to Chase, enjoying the strength of his chiseled arms, the heat of his body, the tenderness in his smile.

Nope. We are absolutely not destined to be the couple who never sees each other and forgets why they fell in love to begin with.

I refuse.

Chapter Seventeen

Jeri

"This morning is harder with you here."

"Uh, ouch." I pinch Chase's ribs.

He smiles. "I'm serious. But not in a bad way. All I want to do is hole away with you, and these meetings are going to feel ten times as boring and lengthy knowing you're out here all by yourself. I tried to get you in, but they're more top secret than the CIA."

It's the hundredth time he's apologized for abandoning me today. I remind myself I prepared for it. I can get used to the busyness. I can. I will. For Chase, I will.

"I know," I tell him. "Don't worry about me. I'm a California girl, remember? I've got this."

I give him my best smile. He eyeballs me for a few seconds. Long enough I start to wonder if he can read my deepest, hidden thoughts. All the spinning, the late phone calls with his people since we've arrived, the packed schedules, is tossing me back into a life where I came up short.

A life that ended with me crushed and broken, picking up the pieces of what once used to be a beautiful life.

"Okay," he finally relents. "But tonight, I'm cooking for you again."

"No arguments here."

The elevator slides open to a hallway decked with palm trees in pots, and a tropical Christmas theme going on across the studio offices.

"Oh, Mr. Thorn," a girl with spiky lavender hair says behind the front desk. "They're waiting for you in suite two."

Chase gives her a quick nod, then turns to me. "You promise—"

"Chase, go," I say, and peck his lips. "I'm going to go wander a bit, probably taste test some coffee, and I'll be back here at two thirty, right?"

"That's what they say. If they start going over, I'll pretend to pass out."

"Solid plan. But make sure they don't call an ambulance. That's just a big bill for a fake emergency."

"Good point. I could get a sudden stomach bug."

"Oh, that'll clear the room. Even better—start asking your characters' opinions on things."

His wide grin makes my legs wobble.

"I think I'm ready. Be prepared to either meet me at the hospital, or the psych ward."

"I'll be waiting." I kiss his lips once more, then release his hands.

Chase waves before stepping into a room halfway down a long hallway.

I turn my smile on the front desk. "Any amazing coffee places close by?"

She chomps on a stick of gum and peers at me over her trendy glasses. "Um, yeah. About two blocks down is a little place called the Bird Cage. It's pretty amazing, if you don't mind live animals. They have a lot of macaws and parrots that fly around."

I grimace. "Sanitary?"

She snickers. "Yeah. They keep the perches on the edges of the dining area. I know it sounds strange, but they're pretty soothing to look at."

Could be a good place to drip out some unique flavors. I pat the top of her desk and nod. "Thanks. I'm Jeri, by the way. I'll probably be coming with . . . with Mr. Thorn a lot."

"Noelle." Her lips twitch with a small smile. "And I figured you'd probably be around after all that. I hope he goes with the character talking excuse."

I laugh and relax. I've grown since the last time I lived in this town and couldn't keep up, become my own woman you could say.

This time around I'm not going to break.

Mental note: Parrot coffee bars are weirdly cool.

The colors, the sounds, the squawking words—even if some parrots cussed like a sailor—was utterly entertaining and I can't wait to take Chase whenever he gets a minute to breathe.

After I tried a bubble tea and wrote a few ideas of exotic flavors involving a lot of papaya, avocado, and coconut, I reacquainted myself with the ins and outs of Southern California. I didn't spend a lot of time in L.A. when I lived here, but it's diverse and busy and fun to people watch.

Lonely and boring without Chase, of course.

Truth be told, I'm not sure I fit here anymore. I miss the mountain snow, and the hum of old beater trucks rumbling down a slow-paced Main Street.

My phone dings as if Silver Creek knows I'm stewing.

Sloan: I've been instructed to let you know Pam has added tea bags to the Honey Pot booth. She also says she'll be sending you an invoice for any expense that might go over the committee budget.

Sloan: Oh, she's coming back for more because I'm not busy or anything and have all day to hear her complaints. Stand by.

I chuckle and watch the three little dots blink for five seconds before a new text comes in.

Sloan: Oh—anticlimactic. She also said that some people are very interested in having you inform Chase that he will always have a standing book booth because his face is too pretty to be angry at. Hope

you're having a blast! Tayla has everything under control. Abs and Emmitt Greer will be helping her. No worries! *heart emoji*

I snort a laugh and tuck my phone into my pocket. Maybe if Chase makes a million dollars on his new book we can buy Pam's love again.

With an hour to spare before Chase is supposed to fake his way out of the meeting, I make my way back up to the eighth floor. My feet hurt, and I have grand plans to sit and read the new chapters Rex Blade sent to my email while I wait.

Noelle chews on the end of her pen, staring at her computer screen when I come back inside.

"I come bearing gifts. Merry Christmas," I say, handing her an extra cup of coffee. I might've gone twice to the Bird Cage.

Her eyes turn to glitter. "You are a gem." She breathes deeply. "I'm about to hit the afternoon crash. I feel like I fell in love with you just now. Is that unprofessional to say? I'm not sure I care, but apologies if it is."

"I'll keep your secret. I'd rather be relaxed than stuffy, don't you think?"

She takes a long sip of the coffee, and hums her pleasure. "Yes. Well, at least in front of you. Thank you for this."

"No problem." I jut my thumb over my shoulder at the chairs behind me. "I'm just going to hang out right there until he's done."

"I'd expect about another hour, there are a few more people coming that might be potential crew. Want to see if everyone jives, you know?"

I nod, but I really don't know this process at all. Chase says he doesn't have much of a say, but they want him as a consultant. What does that mean exactly?

Not my problem to worry about. Noelle busies about making copies, typing, and doing whatever it is she does in a back room behind her desk. I sit, groaning at the delightful relief in my feet, and start to read.

Maybe two minutes later, the door opens again, and an entourage of men and women in fancy clothes, sunglasses, cell phones, and hurried voices burst into the room. My stomach drops.

Is the room getting hotter?

Walls, are they shrinking?

Belle Keys, the actress who plays Revna the pirate, and Brett Bowers the young King Lux step into the room. They whisper to each other, and both look like they're exhausted.

But behind them, standing five feet away from me is a twenty-something, mussed hair, scruffy chinned, Noah Hayden.

The face of young Kage Shade.

In real life, he looks older than the show trailers made him. But movie magic, right? He's playing eighteen-year-old Kage, but I know he's really twenty-three. My palms are sweaty. This is sort of cool. I've never been around a real, A-list actor. When I still went to premiers with Grady, no one knew the names of the actors in his films yet.

Honestly, Noah is only an A-lister thanks to *Wicked Darlings*. Headlines say the show is putting the guy on the map.

I read an article in *People* that Pam shoved in my face when she still loved me last week that said he's a little mysterious. Not much backstory yet. A drama student from LSU in Louisiana, got a start in commercials and a short stint on a soap opera, and apparently he has a semi-famous twin brother, too.

Another soon-to-be-famous Hayden who plays in a rock band in Las Vegas or something.

I don't know, I don't listen to hard rock, but I do have a very invested interest in *Wicked Darlings*, and the people who are turning my favorite books into a success for my favorite author.

I hold my breath, embarrassed the way my brain is freaking out like I'm a high school girl again, as Noah takes the chair three down from me.

He doesn't take off his sunglasses, and keeps his eyes trained on his phone.

Does he get overwhelmed? Or is he a total snob and doesn't notice the world around him? Belle and Brett are still huddled in their corner, chatting about something, but Noah is disconnected from everyone.

I'd like to remind him he wouldn't be famous without Chase—my boyfriend—but I don't need to be petty. I'm a woman who's inching toward thirty-four, and I simply love the show he's part of.

I can tell him that without getting weird.

"Here for the *Wicked Darlings* meeting?"

Noah lifts his eyes off his phone and shoves his sunglasses over his head. Oh, cool, his eyes are two-toned. One is sort of hazel, the other leans closer to blue. Contacts must get his eyes the dark, shadowy brown described in the books.

A smile curls in the corner of his mouth. "Yeah. Are you?"

"Uh, no. Chase Thorn—Rex Blade—he's my boyfriend. I'm just waiting."

"No way." Noah's smile widens, and he adjusts in his seat, so we're talking face to face. He has a little twang of a Southern accent, and I'm even more impressed. I haven't seen the show, but in the trailers he uses a British accent, and he nails it.

"Chase is so down to earth," Noah goes on. "I can't tell you how many calls I've made to the poor guy trying to get the character right, and he's been so helpful. I'm Noah."

He holds out his hand, like I don't exactly who he is.

"Jeri."

"So, Jeri, do you have any—you know—insider information on what happens in the last book?"

I laugh and all at once I'm at ease. "My lips are sealed."

Noah grins, giving away the boyishness of his face. "All right. That was only attempt one. I'm sure I'll try at least a dozen more times to get it out of you."

This is, dare I say, fun. What was I so worried about?

"Jericho?"

Fun. Over.

I jolt. A crease forms in Noah's brow. My face must be bloodless because he looks like he's readying to catch me if I tip over.

Slowly, with a sick twist in my gut, I lift my gaze. No, no, no. This city is huge. We should not be meeting like this. From the back of the suits and sunglasses steps Grady L. Perkins.

I bolt to my feet, chest tight, flight reflex fully engaged.

"Jeri, wow." Grady smirks, shoves his hands in the pockets of his fitted, no doubt disgustingly expensive slacks. His eyes drink me in and not in a good way. Like a shark in a pool of blood. "I'd recognize that body anywhere."

"Whoa. A little over the line. Don't make the lady uncomfortable." Noah stands. Ah, he's cute. He's taking a place between us, like my own personal anti-Grady shield.

Big of him. Directors, producers, writers, they all have the power to fire him off the show. Kage changes, so they could spin it as they needed a different face for the natural aging of the character.

Officially, Noah Hayden and I are friends whether he wants to be or not. But I don't need chivalry right now, I need to get away from my stupid, arrogant ex-boyfriend.

If Grady was intimidated by Noah's white knight attempt, he doesn't show it. Simply claps the actor on the shoulder and chuckles. "Jeri and I go way back. What are you doing here, babe?"

"First, I'm not babe. Second, it's not your business why I'm here."

He grins. Ugh. It's a nasty grin. Sly and unbecoming. What happened to this guy?

At the worst possible moment, Noelle skips out of the back room, cheerful as ever. "Oh, you all are here. Feel free to head on back. Jeri, good you met Mr. Perkins. He might be on the director's team for *Wicked Darlings*."

What? No. Chase couldn't know or he'd lose his mind. Oh, Grady has a surprise waiting for him in there. If Chase even has a say. What if he doesn't? This could ruin his excitement for his own book adaptation!

All at once my parrot coffee isn't sitting well.

"Mr. Perkins," Noelle goes on, "this is Jeri, Mr. Thorn's—" She pauses when she sees my subtle head shake. "Uh, his friend."

Grady goes in for the kill. His smile spreading. Gross—he laughs. In my face. "Ah, Jer, Jer, Jer. I knew you wouldn't stay away for good."

"Thanks, but you don't know anything about me anymore." I look to Noah, forcing a smile. "Pleasure to meet you. Good luck on the next season."

Noah gives me a stiff nod, clearly uncomfortable with the building tension, but he's saved when a blonde woman in a pantsuit gestures to him, Belle, and Brett to follow them back.

I try to leave; I'll wait for Chase outside, but before I can get past, Grady grabs my arm.

"You're with Chase Thorn?"

"Let go," I say.

I close my eyes when Grady lowers his face alongside mine. "Such a small world. Do I even want to know how you ended up with him? Guess it doesn't matter, but I think we'll be seeing a lot of each other soon. Good. I've missed you."

I shirk him off. "Leave me alone, Grady."

"Is there a problem?" Noelle asks with more power in her voice than I expect.

Grady smiles that flashy grin. "No problem. We're old friends." He faces me again. "I'm looking forward to working on this show. It's going to be busy, busy, busy. Lots of press junkets, lots of premier parties. This is really going to launch Chase's face in the spotlight. Sure you can take the late nights, the fans, the attention? Trust me, with me and my people at the head, we'll make sure his life is never the same."

Blood runs out of my face. Grady is just slippery enough that he'd do everything to put Chase out there as a way to get back at me. He'd force the PR departments to demand more press, more author interviews, all to make sure he still has a grip on my life.

"You're still torn up that I left you, huh?" I whisper.

"Not torn up. Simply making a point." He leans closer. "I do the leaving, Jeri."

He's despicable. And now Chase is caught in this mess.

"Leave him alone, Grady. His writing means everything to him, but he doesn't want his personal life invaded."

"Oh, Jer. Of course he does. He's the author and can stay back if he wants. He can write the books while we write the scripts. So, you should ask yourself, why is he here if he doesn't want that life?" Grady starts down the hallway, but turns for his last biting word. "With another book and more seasons this show is about to become the next phenomenon. Chase Thorn hasn't even taken a bite of the fame he's going to experience. Trust me, babe, if you're not up for it, he'll find someone else who is. I'll make sure he handles his fame well."

And there it is—Grady knows how to cut at the ankles, so I lose all my footing.

He's going to hurt Chase. No one will notice it, maybe not even Chase, but I will. Because I left the guy, Grady will take out his jealousy and need to control on the man I love.

Not if I can help it. A tear falls onto my cheek.

"Jeri?" Noelle asks. "Are you okay?"

"Yeah. Um, can you tell me if what he said is true? Is this show going to blow up?"

Noelle gives me a sympathetic smile. "Yeah. I-I think it is. It's the big focus of the studio right now."

Gosh, my heart warms with pride. Chase has accomplished something amazing. *He's* amazing. There's no way I'm going to be a reason his dream might turn into a nightmare.

I wipe the tear away and force a smile. "I'm going to head out. Will you let Chase know I went back to his place?"

"Sure thing."

My heart hurts.

I love Chase. I love him enough not to ruin this for him.

Even if it destroys me.

Chapter Eighteen

Chase

I'm ready to play one of my escape tactics.

"I promise, we're almost done," Tasha whispers. She brushes her long red hair off her shoulder and winks.

"We'll begin production in spring," one of the producers of *Wicked Darlings* says. "Then begin pre-production on season three late fall. I think releasing two seasons fairly close together will keep fans hungry for the next."

The studio's PR executive nods and offers her agreement. "We'll also be pulling in new technical directors for different shots and scenes."

"Why is that?" I ask. "I thought Dimitri did a great job on the first season."

"Dimitri is the performance director," the woman says. "But he'll need assistance as production travels to different sets. The script requires a few specialized shots. It's a good thing when a show needs a larger team to make it shine. An even better thing when a show has the budget to do it."

"And season three will need more hands on," says another producer. "Dimitri has a few more engagements next fall, so he'll need a co-executive."

A knock comes to the door. Rod, the executive producer stands. "Perfect timing. The team should be here now."

He answers the door. The first faces I see are Brett and Belle, both nice enough, but more interested in the film crew than the publishing and book side. But I grin when Noah Hayden comes in. He reminds me of myself, hesitant, and unsure how to find a place in the spotlight.

"Noah," I say, shaking his hand. "Good to see you, man."

"Hey, Chase." He gives me a guarded smile, almost like he wants to tell me something but we're too crowded already. "Looking forward to working with you again. How's the last book coming? I gotta know how you kill me off."

I laugh. The guy is a legitimate fan of the books, and that makes it better that he's playing Kage. Not sure I'd trust the growly assassin with anyone else. I pound a fist over his thigh. "It's coming. Get off my back, you're worse than Tasha."

She clicks her tongue. "Glad there is another one of me to encourage you."

"Is that what we're calling it now?"

Noah chuckles, so does my agent. The few relationships I've built over the course of filming have made this a dream come true. One I feel like is about to change as more people flood into the room. Men, women, executives, directors, a lot of people I don't know. I don't like all the changes; Dimitri and I had a good balance last season. I'd offer input, but he didn't step on my toes and I didn't step on his. I was a bit reclusive since Heather had only died a few months before, but I still appreciated it.

Now I'll need to find a rapport with all these new people to make sure they don't botch *Wicked Darlings* entirely.

"Great, we're all here." Rod says. He starts dishing out some of the rough scripts for season two to the actors. Season two—of my book. I still can't believe it. "Here are some of the opening scenes. Just to give you a feel for the tone we're wanting."

I sit back, checking my phone. It's almost three. Do they need me for this?

Probably. Without fail one of the actors or producers will have a question once the script is pulled out. Up until now, we've reviewed the first scenes, and the screenwriters continue to wow me. I suppose we'll get the actors' take and director feedback on their vision going forward.

One of the new guys sits across from me, staring at me with a weird smile.

The hair raises on my arms.

Noah leans in, script out, and points to a line. "Right here, when you wrote him, what is he thinking?"

I glance at the script, but stop when Noah keeps going.

"I'm going to act like I'm talking to you about the script—and I'll nail it because I'm an actor—but I'm really trying to tell you something else."

"Okay."

"Good, keep looking at the script. So, I met your girl outside. Really nice."

"Yeah, she's awesome. Is that all you wanted to tell me in your weirdly sneaky way?"

"No." He drops his voice even lower. "The guy over there. He knows her; sort of upset her."

My blood chills in my veins.

"Eyes on the script," Noah hisses. "We're acting, man."

It takes all my brain power to keep my eyes pointed at the script. "What's his name?"

"He's a director. Grady Perkins."

Bile teases the back of my throat. This guy, this is the tool who hurt Jeri? Why is he in this room? Another second and it hits me like a bag of books. He's being called up as one of the technical directors.

Not. A. Chance.

"That's her freaking ex," I say through my teeth.

Noah winces. "I probably shouldn't stick my nose in it, but, I don't know, if it was my girl, if I even had a girl, which I don't, but if I did—"

"*Noah.*"

"Sorry, I ramble sometimes. I'm just saying, I would want to know."

There aren't words—at least not ones I can say without bringing shame to my family name. Whatever he said to Jeri . . .

I'm so mad I want to break this guy's nose.

That's my cue to leave.

"Tash," I say, voice rough. "Something came up. My dad fell off a ladder. Christmas lights, can't get the guy to hire out."

I wiggle my phone at her, even though there isn't a message or anything even lighting the screen.

Her eyes go wide. "You're kidding? Um, yeah, go. We're basically finished for today, but tomorrow? You're good, right?"

"Should be. I'll keep you updated." I clap hands with Noah in half high-five, half handshake, then leave the room with a narrowed, boiling glare at Grady Perkins.

He reclines in his chair, arms open. Confident, smug, and before I leave, he winks.

I've tried to call Jeri ten times. She's not answering. How long ago did she leave? Noelle told me she went to my apartment. The car can't go fast enough.

Once I'm there, I wave to my doorman, then take the stairs two at a time instead of waiting for the elevator. I scan the lock with my phone and burst inside. Lights are low. It's quiet.

My heart leaps into my throat when my eyes fall onto Jeri. She's seated at my barstool.

"Jer." I hurry across the room and wrap her in my arms. "Are you okay? I had no idea they were calling him in."

She rests her cheek to my chest, holding me tightly. "I know."

I tighten my hold around her and press a kiss to the top of her head. My pulse slows, my shoulders unclench as if each muscle relaxes one by one.

"But there's something I need to talk to you about."

What I want to do is what I always do—hold her tighter, kiss her senseless, laugh about the irony of life later—but everything about her body language is telling me to keep a bit of distance. She's closed off, and I want to fix it.

I shove my hands in my pockets and nod. "Okay, sure. What's up?"

"I've been thinking a lot today, talking to a lot of people who all have amazing things to say about you, your goals, your growth." She pauses, closes her eyes for a breath. "I've decided to . . . head back to Silver Creek. For the festival. I shouldn't have shirked my responsibilities to begin with."

As if her words are a string, I'm pulled tight in every direction all over again. "Why?"

"This is turning into something huge, Chase," she says. Jeri pulls away, chin tilted, eyes wet. "And I'm so proud of you. But—"

The dreaded *but*. Something happened and my blood won't stop beating against my skull.

"I'm not ready to step back into this life again," she says.

I shake my head. "He did something, said something. Noah Hayden told me he made you uncomfortable."

"Nothing Grady said is a lie. Your life is going to change, and I can't wait to cheer you on. It's just not the life I want, and I promised myself I'd never live life in the background again. There is a reason I moved to Silver Creek, and that reason hasn't changed. My life, my family, my dreams are there. Everything between us is happening so fast, and it's been wonderful, but I think it's wise to take a step back. To figure out if these big changes are something we both want."

"What's to figure out? You like my career, I like yours, we love each other—"

"But your life is about to explode in ways I'm not sure you even see, yet. And you deserve to live it; you've earned it. I'm so proud of you."

I take another step back. "Proud, but don't want anything to do with it, right?"

"I-I'm not sure what I want right now. It's all been so fast, and frankly, I'm scared." She hesitates. Her chin trembles and pools of tears well in her eyes. "I'm not cut out for this life, and I'd never ask you to pump the brakes on your success to appease me."

"So what are you asking? What are you saying, Jeri?"

"I'm saying, I'm going to go back to Silver Creek. I think it's best if we do this now before we—"

"Before what? Before I fall in love with you? Too late, Jer." I pound a fist to my chest. "This thing, it's already yours."

She lowers her gaze to the floor, wiping at her eyes.

I keep waiting for her to look at me, to get to the end where she pulls me in, and I tell her she doesn't need to worry. Where I assure her I'm hers. Where my touch, my kiss, can convince her I'll never be Grady.

But she slings the strap of her bag over her shoulder, wipes her eyes, and looks at me with words on the tip of her tongue. Words I hate and I haven't even heard them yet.

"Jeri, my life isn't going to change," I say a throaty whisper. "I'm still doing the same thing I've always been doing. Writing books. I'm hardly a decision maker when it comes to the show. Noah, Belle, Brett—those guys are the ones who'll be in the spotlight."

She opens her mouth, but hesitates. When she does speak, there is a quiver buried underneath her confidence. "Exactly. You don't have a say on much as an author. But they'll have a say in what you need to do. Contracts that say do this, or do that, and you deserve to live this, Chase. You deserve to have the rewards from all your work."

"I don't want it. I want you."

"For how long?" She shakes her head almost like she didn't mean to say it. "This has been exhilarating, fun, and some of the best weeks of my life. But we've been living in a bubble in the mountains. How long will I still be fun and exciting when you're brushing shoulders with the elite?"

I narrow my eyes. "You're putting me in the same box as Grady right now. Don't make me pay for his stupid mistakes."

"I'm not," she says. "I'm trying to make the best choice. This is your life, and it's incredible. But I left this pace for a reason. You deserve someone who wants to run with you."

I press a hand to my chest. My heart burns like it's cracking down the middle. When did this go off the rails? "So, what? You never leave Silver Creek?"

"Am I supposed to uproot my life? Are you? For something that started a few weeks ago?"

It's a shot to the gut. For a second I try to hold back, try to keep calm, but it feels like the walls are crumbling in and I let go.

"Stop making excuses we both know you don't mean. You're afraid I'm going to be him—but the key word there is afraid. I'm not him, Jericho. I'm not. I don't aspire to be him, I don't want press, and spotlight, and a woman on each arm. I want you more than I want books, more than I want a TV show. Tell me what I need to do to prove it to you, to show you that nothing else matters. I love you, and I don't care if it happened in two weeks, or if it happened in two days! Who gets to set a timeline for us? We do. I'm not going to be that guy who ditches you or hurts you, and I'm asking you to give me a chance to prove it to you."

I take a breath. Never been one to talk big, and I think I spit out more words in one breath than I ever have in my life. There's a heady silence that fills the space. My pulse won't stop racing. My heart, it won't stop aching.

"Chase," her voice cracks and she takes my arm.

"Be honest, Jer. What did he say?"

Her big, wet eyes break my heart into a thousand pieces. "Is it enough to trust me when I say it'll be better for you if I'm not around for all this?"

The guy is dead. He's freaked her out and I'm standing here like a net with a thousand holes watching her slip through my fingers.

Jeri touches my arm. "I'm not asking you to change anything, or wait for me to figure things out, or anything. I just think this is for the best."

A fist squeezes my lungs. I'm not going to go down this road again. Falling fast, hard, deep, then getting decimated in the end. She's really leaving.

"When? When do you go?"

"I'm taking a shuttle to Utah, then to Denver. Rowan or Sloan will pick me up."

I step around her, afraid if I touch her I'll never let her leave. But I will move aside because what else can I do? I know a thing or two about living in the shadows of the past, and no one can convince her anything will be different this time around but herself.

I clear my throat and look out the window. "Will you let me know you made it safely?"

"Yes," she whispers.

My defenses are up. I look at the ground for few breaths, then nod, and go for my bedroom. My world feels like a deep, harsh crack is splitting it in pieces. I don't stop. It hurts too much. It *burns*. Different from when Heather died, but truth be told, just as fierce.

I pace behind my bedroom door, fingers in my hair. The ground tilts, but surprisingly, my head clears. Grady unraveled her defenses she's so carefully built since she abandoned city life for a smaller, simpler existence. Obviously.

She's afraid. I am too. But there is no way I'm not following through with what I said.

Book deal, TV deal, or not, I make grand plans to show Jericho Hunt she is the first thing my heart beats for in the morning, and she always will be.

Chapter Nineteen

Chase

My fists clench and unclench. I stand outside the conference room door, intentionally late. I want to make sure everyone is in the room.

Another breath, another second, and I step into the room.

The studio's PR woman lifts a penciled brow. Tasha taps her wrist even though she's not wearing a watch. I do a quick scan of the room, making sure everyone is here, then sit at the table.

"Sorry I'm late," I bite out, careful to avoid the smug stare coming from the end of the table. "Personal things."

"No problem," Rod says with a smile. "You came at the perfect time. We were just discussing the terms of your consultation. Noah, what were you saying?"

Noah glances at me from across the thick table. "You're invaluable, Chase. I think I speak for Belle, and Brett, too, when I say you've helped us shape these characters. Personally, I think that's why it's exploding. Viewers who are also the book lovers are completely satisfied."

"Yeah, for sure," Belle Keys says in her sing-song voice. "We all know how picky bookish people can be with their adaptations. It's been really helpful, Mr. Thorn."

I give a nod of thanks, but gesture to Rod. "I can't take much credit. These guys produced the show, and you all are the ones who brought the characters to life."

"With your help," Brett says through a yawn. Tabloids say he's a bit of a party boy, but at least he's coherent.

"That's all we're saying," Noah adds. "Your consultation and input helped us get into the heads of these characters, and I think it's created a satisfying show for non-readers and readers alike."

"Right," Rod says, scrubbing his hands together. "Because of it, we're looking to make you a fulltime consultant on the show. The shots, settings, and arcs are getting trickier and bigger. Another reason we're bringing in a few more heads to bounce ideas with." He gestures to the few directors and assistants.

I still don't look at Grady. Not yet.

"Chase, what do you think?" Tasha asks. "This can be a new worldwide show. They're calling it the next *Game of Thrones*."

What do I think? Back-to-back seasons as a fulltime consultant would take up a huge chunk of my life. Exactly what Jeri didn't want.

I love Jeri. She opened my heart and took it for her own over a matter of weeks. My heart is blue and black, and more than a little broken since our last conversation. But underneath her reluctance, I'm going out on a limb to say there is a hefty bit of her own fear and insecurity in there.

At the end, I could see how she convinced herself she was doing this to protect me. Whatever Grady threatened, whatever he told her would happen latched on tight. Jeri lived in a comfortable sense of security in Silver Creek. Those mountains and trees kept her safe from the heartbreak of her busy, flashy past. She didn't want to leave the safety of it.

I can understand.

How long have I lived in the secure, familiar fog of grief and a promise that's become wretchedly impossible to keep?

In the weeks after Heather's death, somewhere in my own head I found complacency, a new normal. But meeting Jeri upset it all. Her laughter, her kisses, her touch, broke through the heavy gates I'd placed around my comfort zone, and yanked until I stumbled out.

Is it so hard to believe she unconsciously did the same?

An ache blooms behind my eyes. I found something rare in Silver Creek, and it's broken right now.

But to fix it is worth everything.

Being back here, the longer I stare at the busy city feeling alone in the world, the more I realize this place isn't my home. It hasn't been for a long time.

Home for me looks like gossip over coffee, neighbors who peek in your windows and call your name instead of knocking on the door, waving at anything that moves because you'd hate to mistakenly ignore someone you know. Here, I feel like I'm out of place and searching for anything warm to hold to and coming up empty.

Now, I plan to prove it.

I stand, leaning over the table on my fingertips. "I've spent the last decade of my life in these books. To be here is a dream. I can't thank everyone enough for the amazing work you've done to bring *Wicked Darlings* to life. To continue, is all I want. I want nothing but success for this show and these books, but I will not be a consultant in the least if Grady Perkins is a director on this show."

The room falls into a rotten silence. Rod gapes at his producers. Whispers ripple through the publishing team. Noah bites his bottom lip. Truth be told, it looks like he's trying not to laugh. Belle and Brett shrink in their seats a bit.

I point my stare at Grady.

He returns it with a glare of his own. "What's the trouble, Mr. Thorn? We've never even spoken before."

"And it's still too much," I say, my face pulled in a smug smile. I look back to Rod. "I'm not going to go into details, but I won't work with him for my own reasons. Now, I'm only a consultant, rights have been sold, so the show can go on without me. But those are my terms. I step back if he's brought on."

"You're putting us in a hard sport, Chase," Rod says.

"I wish I wasn't, truly, but nowhere in my contract does it say I must be part of this show."

"But we need you," says a squirrely woman. One of the writers. "It's been an entirely different vibe to work so, so, *so* closely with the author. The proof is in the numbers! Fans are expecting the same for the next four seasons. *Four seasons*, Mr. Thorn!"

I step back from the table, glancing at Tasha who looks like she might pass out. "I'm moving. I'll send you my change of address forms and new contact information."

"Chase what's going on?"

"I'll talk to you about it later."

"This is ridiculous," Grady says. "Let the man go if he wants."

I dip my chin and turn for the door.

"Chase, wait," Rod says, jolting out of his seat. "Let's discuss this, see what we can compromise.

Reps from my publisher, and a few of the studio producers shift in their seats. I get it, my stomach is coiled into hard, thorny knots, but I'm not backing down. With a pointed look, I cross my arms over my chest, eyeballing Rod with a new determination.

"Those are my terms. I'm not compromising. So, what is it going to be, Rod? The ball is in your court."

He pauses, looks around the room, as if someone will pop up and tell him what to do.

All I can do is stand there with one foot out the door, and wait.

It'll be dark soon.

This has been the moment I've avoided all day. I've used packing, arranging with my doorman to have the rest of my things moved over the next week, as excuses to stay away.

But I can't avoid this anymore.

The cemetery is quiet. Headstones are marked in poinsettias or small spruce trees. Some have Christmas stars or Nativity scenes from loved ones who'll miss them. I fiddle with the large, gold ornament that will hang from the shepherd's crook.

Heather loved the simplicity of gold at Christmastime.

Throat tight, I make my way down the row until her upright, dark glossy headstone comes into view. A coal of pain stirs in my chest. The granite is covered in solar Christmas lights and a small wreath. I swallow the scratch in the back of my throat and lower to a crouch.

On instinct, my fingers trace the lines and curves of her name.

"Hey, Heath. I've been gone for a while; sorry I haven't stopped by. A lot has happened, and I know we didn't like to talk about work, but I'm writing again. Oh, and I think I just broke the studio too. Surprising, right? You always said I had a rebellious side somewhere in me, and I think it came out." Silence builds. So does the sting behind my eyes. In a way this feels like losing her all over again, and in the same breath it's as if she's here, like I could reach out and touch her. "I'm, uh, I'm leaving L.A., but I couldn't go without seeing you again."

I wipe the heel of one hand over my eyes.

"Heath." My voice cracks. "I . . . miss you. I hope you know that, and I think I'll always miss you. The sticky notes—" I let out a little chuckle. "Even if you were mad at me, I knew I could find those sticky notes with your little stick figures every morning telling me to have a great day. The late night talks. Freaking Monopoly. You cheated, and you know it."

My stomach tightens as I rest one hand on the frigid stone. "I miss you, but the pain . . . it's starting to dull more and more. You're becoming a memory, and I don't, I don't know how to feel about it. It feels like I'm betraying you on one hand, then on the other it feels like it's what should happen, I guess."

Another pause. I imagine her face, her smile. The air isn't so cold anymore. Heat spreads in my chest, as if she's pressing her hand there, adding a bit of comfort to the heartbreak.

Tears come. I don't try to stop them. My grip tightens on the top of her headstone as I kneel. "Heath, I made you a promise and—" My eyes squeeze shut. "I can't keep it. I . . . fell in love with someone. I didn't see it coming, but you always said I zoned out too much."

I laugh, then pretend she's laughing with me. The headstone blurs as more tears come. My voice lowers to a whisper, hardly audible over the winter breeze.

"I loved you the best I could. I never expected our story to end this way." I run my sleeve under my nose. The cold, the tears, it's running and won't stop. "I thought we'd be living in the suburbs, maybe have a little you and me by now. You'd give me the look when I put empty cereal boxes back in the pantry, and I'd still be eating all those burned casseroles with a smile. I thought that was it, that was the happily ever after, but life sucks sometimes.

"I'm sorry I couldn't keep my promise." I pause, the hair lifts on the back of my neck. Not in a creepy way, but in the same she-feels-close way. "But I have a feeling you probably didn't think I'd keep it. I'll never forget you, though. You taught me what it meant to really love someone else. You were the first to hold my heart, and you'll always have a piece of it."

I press a kiss to my fingertips, then touch her name.

Warmth and peace settles in my chest. Why have I avoided this? It's as if a door is finally closing on a festering wound, but it doesn't sting like I thought. There isn't an image of Heather hating me wherever she is right now, more like she's rolling her eyes and saying, "It's about time, dummy."

"Chase?"

I startle at my name and whip around, embarrassed by the tear tracks on my face.

Blood pounds in my head as I furiously swat at my eyes to wipe away the wetness. "Marcia. Hi."

Heather's mother gives me a soft, sympathetic smile. In her hands she's holding new Christmas décor, and a little solar lantern to light the grave at night.

"Sweetheart, it's been so long." She opens her arm and squeezes my neck. "How are you?"

"I'm good. Sorry, I should've . . . I should've come around a little more. I've been out of town."

"Oh, I know. We've been following all the book news, big shot." Marcia nudges my ribs with her elbow, then starts to settle her things around Heather's grave.

My chest cinches. "Marcia, I . . . I'm moving. I won't be around much anymore, but if you ever need anything, don't hesitate to call me."

She turns over her shoulder. There is pain in her eyes, but a smile on her lips. "I think that's good, Chase. I really do."

I didn't expect that. "You do?"

"Honey, you've been stuck since Heath left us. We've all been worried about you, and I think a change of scenery is just the ticket."

My voice chokes in the back of my throat. "I'm moving because I . . ."

How do I admit what's been going on? This is Heather's *mother*.

I shudder when her hand falls to my arm. She looks at me with tears in her eyes. "You met someone?"

"I didn't expect to."

Her lips curl into a smile. "No one ever does, do they?"

"I promised her she'd be it for me," I say pointing at Heather's headstone.

"Oh, Chase, she'd be so mad at you if you followed through with that." Marcia places one of the decorations next to my ornament, then narrows her eyes at me. "Heather loved you, and it helps heal a bit of my broken heart knowing she got to experience the real, giddy, forever kind of love before she died. You gave her that, but she'd want you to be happy down here. She told me."

"What?"

"Honey, I had a lot of talks with my girl when we knew—" Marcia pauses when her voice cracks. "When we knew it wasn't going to end the way we wanted. She told her dad and me to look after you, to encourage you to keep writing and keep going. To be happy, Chase. The thought of you being alone and hurting was really her only worry. It's okay to move on. Doesn't mean you've forgotten her, sweetie."

She's crying. I'm crying. It's a mess, but when she hugs me, when she lets me squeeze her back, it's like a weight lifts off my shoulders. I'll swear until the day I die, I felt Heather hugging us right back.

When we pull ourselves together, wiping our eyes, laughing a little sheepishly, Marcia squeezes my hand. "You'll always be part of our family. We're happy for you. So is Heather."

By the time dusk settles over the cemetery, we walk out together, and grab coffee. She fills me in on what is going on with Tom, her husband, and his retirement. Heather's two sisters—one is in college, the other is probably going to be married by summer. She asks about Jeri. I tell her the story, the surprise way another woman took my love; I even admit the blow up at the end.

"Go get her, Chase," Marcia says outside. "If she's the woman who deserves you, she'll be there. Of course, I expect to meet her someday."

I hug her again, hoping she will meet Jeri, then I leave, lighter, and freer than before. Now, I'm hoping I'm not too late to fix what I left back home.

Home. I'm going *home*.

Chapter Twenty

Jeri

"You okay?" Sloan leans against the doorjamb, two mugs in hand.

I lift my head off the chill of the window. Truth be told, I hadn't realized somewhere during the baked apple breakfast crisp, I'd zoned out and stared at the falling snow instead of stirring the caramel sauce.

Great. Now the kitchen of Holly Berry smells like scorched pan bottom. I curse under my breath and turn off the burner. I could blame the haze on a twenty-four-hour total shuttle ride with too many pitstops to count, or that the festival is today and will start in ten hours. But that isn't the half of it.

"Sorry, nugget," I say to Sloan's stomach. "Bet that was stinky for you."

Sloan sniffs one of the mugs. "We're covered."

"I'll put in one of the breakfast casseroles from the freezer," I say. "No worries, guests will be satisfied."

Angel will be here soon, and he'll be able to add a spin on a boring breakfast.

"You aren't on duty. You're not even supposed to be cooking. Besides, I'm not worried about food, I'm more worried about you," she says when I'm half buried in the freezer.

Sloan hands me a second mug. Peppermint tea. A staple for Sloan lately, and my heart tightens. It's nice to be thought of. Sort of like when a man cooks for you even though you're a chef, and he does a really good job, and . . .

Ah, now I understand the spacing off. My head falls to the countertop as though thoughts of Chase grow too heavy to keep upright.

"Jer, what happened?" Sloan asks.

"I told you," I say, a tremble in my voice. "My past came back to bite him."

"I know that's what you said, but did *he* agree?"

"He doesn't know Grady. I do. He's like a dog with a brutal, jagged, mean bone."

"Yeah, and he played on your fear of losing a guy to the rush of fame. He's jealous and a total jerk. But Chase is not even close to Grady."

My heart stills. Not in a good way. In a hot, sharp, blinding kind of pain.

I whimper and let my head fall again. I love Chase. I love him unconditionally. There are no expectations he doesn't meet, couldn't meet. I love his laugh. His wit. I love his creativity. His delicious face. When he showed vulnerability in his work, I couldn't get enough. The way he trusted me, inspired me, and brightened *every single day*.

But if me being there caused this to turn into something awful, well, I had to leave. Right?

"Jeri." Sloan strokes my hair. "Girl, talk to me."

"I'm comfortable here!" I cover my face with my palms. "I'm happy. I have a life here. I have you, and Ro, and Abs."

"But is it enough?" she asks. "Without Chase, is it enough?"

"He's everything." I groan and let my head flop back onto the countertop.

"Then quit giving some putz with an ego the size of Alaska all this power. You think we wouldn't still be here if you went on an adventure with a super sexy guy who wants to spend his massive wallet on you and love you hard? Hire Tayla as your manager, hire some more day help, travel to his big parties, come back and drink coffee and make me cinnamon rolls, then go to premiers in fancy dresses. You can have it all. Chase is looking nowhere but at you, girl. We all saw that."

I snort a wet laugh. "You're annoying when you make sense."

"I know. My rightness miffs Rowan a lot too." Sloan grins and adjusts in her seat. "Jer, level with me. What's the real issue here?"

Tears blur the room. I hang my head. "I love him so much, Sloanie. The thought of anything from my life ruining his, or breaking his heart, or changing his dreams, made me sick. Grady has connections; he has power as a director, and could lock Chase into something he hated."

I wince, sickened how my ex somehow weaseled into my subconscious, so I've possibly destroyed something sweet and beautiful and perfect. "How long before it happens again, anyway? The fame, the expectations. The extra *company*."

"The difference is Chase is already there," Sloan says softly. "Jeri, you realize that right? He's already famous. So what if the show blows up, is that suddenly going to make Mr. Cabin-in-the-Woods author want to jump in front of cameras on a red carpet? I mean, this is Chase we're talking about. The guy who clams up anytime someone mentions his pseudonym."

I laugh at that, wiping my eyes. "He does get shy when people find him out, doesn't he?"

"Yeah," Sloan says, her smile widening. "Not to mention that heartbreaking fact that you told me he's basically been in a grief-stricken writer's block over his fiancée. Does that sound like a guy who'll jump a bunch of models and leave the woman he loves at home to cry? I understand he's a risk in your head, but I also understand what can happen when you take those risks. Even if they've burned you before. I really do."

She does. Rowan was her first love, but he hurt her. Yet, she's married to the guy who was a risk, with a kid, and another one on the way. And her risky guy gets to find out about baby number two in two more days. I saw the giftbag, and I know Rowan will turn into a blubbering mess.

Chase could be that guy. We could be that way. What am I so afraid of? Why did I give Grady so much power? I fiddle with the ends of my hair. "I've thought of calling him a thousand times. I don't know, it feels too little too late."

"Nah. The way you two light up around each other, being honest is never going to be too late."

Would he listen? Does he even want to? The hurt in his face stings my memory. I promised him support, then snatched it away, over what? Fear this might rock my perfectly comfortable little life?

For him, no mistake, I'd capsize the entire boat. But I pushed him away to protect a material dream.

He grabbed onto my heart, and I've never wanted him to let go. Not once. He took the risk on me, opening himself when he'd been shutoff for so long. It's a heavy weight to manage, knowing I'd stomped over his vulnerable heart, then made it seem like I hardly cared for him at all.

I rub the bridge of my nose, letting the tears fall without shame.

Sloan slips off the stool and hugs my shoulders. "Don't give it up so easy, and not because some loser left you jaded. Chase is the real deal, Jer. I wouldn't be pushing so hard if I didn't think so."

"You sure it's not because you want an in with the guy who's behind your favorite show?"

"Details," she says with a wave of her hand, then hugs me tighter. "Seriously, though, it's because you've had a new kind of happy in those eyes the last few weeks, and so did Chase. It's a rare look, you know. And you two found it in each other. Those things ought to be fought for."

Before I get the chance to respond, a heavy, furious knock rattles the back door.

"Jericho! Jericho! I know you're in there."

Sloan and I share a look, then both cover our mouths to muffle laughter.

"Is that Pam?" Rowan comes into the kitchen, hair on end, still in sweatpants and a T-shirt. He looks like he's half asleep. "She's been knocking on all the doors. If she wakes up any guests, she's covering their bills."

"Jericho! This is not funny." Pam rattles the door again. "We need to talk!"

I roll my eyes. Welcome back to Silver Creek where the busybodies roam, and gossip feeds the flowers.

I only wish Chase were here to laugh about it with me.

I wonder if my obituary will write *death by dagger eyes*.

Pam hasn't spoken to me since she bombarded the inn this morning. After she discovered it was only me who returned and not her golden boy, she turned her vendetta against me into scowls and the occasional grunt.

Something I thought I'd appreciate, but truth be told, it's terribly unsettling when the woman gets quiet.

There she stands across the square, eyes narrowed, arms folded over her plump chest. Those eyes cut to the core, enough I shudder beneath her disdain.

To say she blames me for the departure of her local star is an understatement.

Her mood is tangible, a physical thing we all can reach out and touch. I take a guess that's the exact reason everyone putting the final touches on their booths or attractions keeps a nice distance from the committee chairwoman.

With a rough swallow, I force myself to look away from my new nemesis and focus on the last few things at my table.

"Don't let her poison my drinks," I tell Tayla.

The woman snorts a laugh. "Emmitt will be on guard duty. No worries. We've got this."

Emmitt, a high school senior who insisted he needed the extra cash, gives me a lazy salute.

The Honey Pot is handling several different flavors for the festival, and it'll be busy. Especially when temperatures really drop after dark. But I think these two will handle it fine.

Maybe Sloan is right. Tayla has been with me since the beginning. She knows the ins and outs of the Honey Pot as well as me. Giving up a bit of control could free up my life in a big way. A way that might help me gather the guts to step out of my comfort zone and follow a super sexy author around while he takes over the world. Even if I have to face my ex-boyfriend on the set of *Wicked Darlings*.

I can do that for Chase. I will do that if he'll have me.

In my text box, I have a full of feelings, pour my heart out, text ready to be sent. A lot of professions of love, need, longing. Promises that I'm behind him one hundred percent.

But it won't be sent.

No. Some words need to be said face to face.

The only trouble is the guy is gone. I'm intent to grand gesture the heck out of him, though, and tell him all the things I should've said that fateful night ten years ago. Or two days ago. Time certainly feels like decades have gone by since I kissed the man, or touched him, or laughed with him, or held him.

All the things with him.

My heart burns a little; a pain I can't sate unless I see Chase Thorn. The entire three years I was with Grady, I never had such need for him like I do a man I met not even a month ago.

I've never been a huge believer in fate, love at first sight, or soul mates. But if I did, I'm just saying Chase would fit the bill.

"Okay." I say. "I think that's everything."

"You've got this," Tayla says, squeezing my hand.

"Do I? Or am I really creating more drama in his life than he needs, and —"

"I can try to break into his apartment lock, Jeri." Abigail, yes little future spy Abigail, materializes with her tablet glowing in her hands. "I've been watching these YouTube videos from a computer genius in Nevada, and I think I could figure it out. Then you could surprise him."

"Abs," I say a little astonished. "Why do you even want to know how to do that?"

"It's cool. I don't really know how." She glances back and forth, then leans in, and whispers. "Yet."

This girl. She's either going to be a tech billionaire or wind up in jail.

I chuckle and ruffle her knit cap. "Don't hack any doors, Abs. Not without your mom and dad's permission, at least."

Tomorrow I have a spot booked on the shuttle. But I'm not staying at the festival. I'm going home to pack. I'm going after the man who holds every piece of my soul, and I've never been so nervous, so thrilled, and so at peace.

I have three different speeches planned for different scenarios. Hopefully, he'll be impressed with my author-esque skills.

Bottom line, I'm going to prove to Chase Thorn he matters.

He matters so much more than whatever Grady Perkins dishes out. My ex doesn't have a say in our lives, and I should've given *us* more credit.

"Wish me luck," I say, and turn to leave for my house.

"Good luck!" rings out from the Honey Pot booth.

I blow out a shaky breath. Okay. I'm doing this. I dodge the thickening crowd, and maneuver to a supply tent in the back of the square. Strands of Christmas lights are stacked in boxes. Extra ornaments, foam cups, first aid supplies, and children's books for Cookie Tinsel to read. I trace one of the books. Poor Bruce—he was not pleased that he'd be donning his old elf tights again. The lumberjack might hate me as much as Pam does right now. I'll make it up to them. Hopefully.

I reach under a long fold-up table and snatch my purse, but when I turn out of the tent, I smash into another body.

"Oh, sorry." Sloan says. "I was coming to find you. I know you're in a rush, and I am all for it. However, there is a teensy, tiny issue in the children's tent. The committee is wondering if you can help before you leave."

Ugh. I let out a groan. "Babe, I really don't—"

"Two minutes, I swear," Sloan says. "I'll fight anyone who tries to get you to stay longer. But it's—"

"Pam. Yeah. The woman is out to bury me. If I disappear after tonight, you know who done it."

I grumble a few thoughts about the grudge-holding busybody, and follow Sloan. I don't want to be in the children's tent. The children's tent is where Cookie Tinsel is supposed to sit on his tufted stool and tell awe-inspiring tales. Bruce will glare at me, and it will destroy the magic for the kids who've started to filter in now that the festival is kicking off.

Sloan links arms with me since I've started dragging my feet. As she pulls back the big canopy flap, I frown; my displeasure at the interruption *will* be made known.

"But Dopey the elf had to escape the goblin nest. Elves don't belong with goblins, you see. And these goblins, well, they looked nice but had sinister plans."

"What plans?" a hushed, child's whisper follows.

"They stole the Princess of Magic Cocoa and drove Dopey away. But he fought them, because there was a very, very important message he needed to deliver to the princess."

I can't breathe.

My mind is blank. Doesn't know how to form a single thought except one.

Chase is sitting on the tufted stool. In a blue tailcoat, tight hose, and the green Cookie Tinsel hat on his head.

He's here. I think he's here. Could be experiencing a strange sort of grief and have manifested his face over Bruce's, but when Sloan releases me it hits. He is here. He's surrounded by kids. Parents are filming. It looks like there is a reporter. Why is a reporter here? One word—Pam.

"How did he get free?" a little boy shouts.

Chase lifts his eyes. His dark, golden gaze locks on me, melting my insides like chocolate. The slightest curl of a smile lights up his face. He turns back to the kids, eyes expressive, hands helping tell the story.

"Dopey learned there was a spell cast over him. But when he broke free, he shouted the magic words to curse the goblins, and then had to flee through a shadow forest. He needed to bid farewell to a lost friend before he could ever return whole to the Princess of Magic Cocoa.

"The shadows tugged, and pulled, and tried to steal away all the Christmas magic that would take him home, but—" He pauses. Kids naturally lean forward, waiting. "There at the end of the shadows was the lost friend. She told Dopey if he didn't return to deliver his message, he'd be, well, he'd be dopey."

A few giggles come from his audience. I hug my middle. Why is he here? Does it matter? I need to touch him in three seconds or I'm going to explode.

"His friend said he always had the power of Christmas magic to return to the Magic Cocoa Kingdom." Chase taps the side of his head. "He just needed to believe it here." His hand moves to his chest. "And here. Because if he didn't believe it, then the princess wouldn't believe his message either.

"Then, all at once, the shadows started to swirl, and swirl, and swirl like a tornado. Then Dopey was flung into the sky, and before he knew it, he landed back in the Cocoa Kingdom."

"Did he find the princess?" asks a little girl, her chin propped on the tops of her knees.

Chase looks to me again. "He did."

When he doesn't go on the little girl sighs. "What happened!"

"Well, I have a secret." Chase points at me, and whispers, "she's the Princess of Magic Cocoa."

My face heats when a dozen little eyes find me.

"Miss Jeri?"

"Yep." Chase stands. "And, as Cookie Tinsel, my buddy Dopey the elf sent me to deliver the last of his message."

"Miss Jeri, he has the message!" A little boy named Rhys shoots to his feet and points at Chase as if I can't see him.

I see him fine. All six foot two, broad, delicious bit of him.

I can't move. My arms tighten around my stomach as Chase starts to cross the room to me. He's sort of blurred. Tears are building, and it's all I can do not to break down in front of our curious audience.

Chase stops a foot away from me. He's too far. I roll my bottom lip between my teeth, lifting my wet gaze.

"I do have a message. On behalf of Dopey, of course."

"Right," I say. My voice comes out breathless. "For Dopey."

Chase takes a step closer. "He's wondering, Princess of Magic Cocoa, if you will allow him to leave all the goblins behind, and help spread Christmas magic with your magic cocoa. I have definitely used the word magic too many times in the same sentence. But he also wanted me to tell you, there is no way he'd choose goblins and all their jewels over a princess like you."

He's close enough if I wanted, I could reach out and touch him. That's exactly what I do.

My hands travel up his chest, curling around his embroidered lapels, like I might be able to stop him if he started to disappear. "I'll answer yours—Dopey's—question with a question. Does he want to return to the kingdom?"

Chase uses a knuckle to lift my chin. "More than anything."

I lean into him; everyone else fades away. "Then I would welcome him back to the kingdom with open arms. Tell him, I'd follow him to *any* kingdom. Even if wicked goblins try to cast nasty spells."

Chase sort of dips his face like he might kiss me, but he pauses. With a glance over his shoulder, he smiles at the kids. "Dopey asked me to kiss the princess if she welcomed him back. It finishes the spell, so close your eyes."

He turns back to me amidst a few groans and giggles. With a smile, he lowers his mouth to mine. I can't help myself, and cling to his neck like he's my lifeline. Chase kisses me with a new desperation. His hands trap my face, holding me there. I kiss him and kiss him and kiss him in all the ways I should've been kissing him.

When we pull apart, the adults clap their approval. Kids gag, and Pam Tilby (who arrived midway during the story) dabs at her eyes.

"I love you," he whispers. "I mean Dopey loves you."

"I love him," I say, burying my face in his neck.

"I think the princess and Cookie need a little time to, uh, deliver another top-secret message," Sloan says, beaming. "But good news, the cookie bar is ready!"

My friend guides us to a separate room in the heated children's tent in time to avoid the stampede of kids rushing to the booths as the festival opens in all its Christmas glory.

A second later, Chase kisses me with more passion than appropriate for a kid audience. I sigh into him, holding a firm grip around his waist. His warmth, his taste, his rustic clean scent, sends my senses into an overload. My body practically screams, *He's here! Celebrate. Celebrate. Celebrate!*

When he pulls back, we're breathless, a little more disheveled, but the smile on my face is there to stay.

Chase rests his forehead to mine and closes his eyes. He opens his mouth to say something, but I interrupt.

"I was coming to you," I blurt out. "I have another shuttle booked for tomorrow—I'm really starting to hate shuttles. I'm sorry, Chase. I'm so sorry for letting him get to me, for making you hurt, even for a little while. I freaked out, but the truth is, I don't care how famous you are. I just want to be with you."

Somehow I spit it all out in a single breath. I only stop when he presses a slow, gentle kiss to my lips.

"I want to be here, Jer. With you. You're my plot twist, you're my new story. I wouldn't have it any other way."

"I wouldn't have you any other way. I shouldn't have let the past get in my head."

"I get it, Jer. I had to let go too."

I stroke the side of his face, breathing him in. "Never stop talking about your books, or your ideas. It's one of those things I love so much about you.

He grins. "I won't, but speaking of my books, I did something. Pretty bold, to be honest."

"What?"

"I refused to consult if Grady was a director."

My eyes go wide. "You didn't?"

"Oh, I did. And if you would've seen it, you would've found me incredibly sexy."

"Already do. What happened?"

"It sort of caused a stir. Grady insisted I be pushed out, so the studio—"

"Chase!" Blood drains from my face.

He grins. "They're looking for another director."

"You're kidding. He's out?"

"He's out. Not sure if it was me who made them choose, or if it was when Noah Hayden insisted he'd leave the show if a guy who harasses women directs it. That set Belle Keys off—she's a huge women's rights activist—so, he's out, Jer."

I'm breathless. "Noah, everyone, they all stood with you?"

"All of them. Well, I think Brett fell asleep, but that's fine, it didn't matter. Now, I'm consulting, and the show is set for at least four more seasons. Although, I did tell them most of my consulting will be done virtually. Turns out I really want to live like a mountain man in a cabin for the foreseeable future."

"Chase don't do this just because I freaked out. I'll go anywhere you need to go. I promise."

He smiles and presses a kiss to my nose. "I know you will, and that means more than I can say. But I wasn't lying. This is home. I want it to be our home. And yes, after the shock wore off, they were fine with it. I might have to fly out a few times a year to work on the show, but that's it. The beauty of being a writer, I guess."

"I'm hiring Tayla as my manager," I say, fast and furious again.

"Really?"

I nod. "I want to live this life with you, and if that means jetting off to fabulous places with your delightful face, I mean, I'd be insane not to. But it also means I need to be a responsible business owner and have someone competent to handle the store. I'm still embarrassed it took me so long to get that in my head."

He kisses me again. I don't know how long it lasts, only that when it ends my face is hot and my legs are weaker.

"I love you, Jericho."

"I love you."

All I can think before he pulls me into him again is thank goodness for wild snowballs.

Jeri

The Holly Berry Inn is decked in twinkling lights in gold, white, and aqua. Not the usual Christmas décor, but Sloan, Loo Graham, Pam, my cousins, and other ladies have spent weeks swapping the garland and lights to prepare for tonight.

When you meet the love of your life in a heap of snow and silver bells, a wedding at an inn that breathes Christmas is the obvious choice.

I lean my head against Chase's shoulder as we finish bits and pieces of the massive wedding cake. All around our friends and family celebrate. Behind the inn the massive tent keeps out the small flurry, and expertly concealed heaters keep the canopy as warm as Holly Berry.

Chase wraps an arm around my shoulders, pulling me closer, and presses a kiss to my forehead. The cool metal of his new ring on my skin sends a jolt to my heart.

We must be on the same wavelengths because he rolls the round diamond on my hand, and smiles. "I like this."

"I like you."

"I hope so. You just married me."

I laugh and kiss the scruff on his chin.

Hard to believe a year and a week ago a rogue ice ball landed me in the arms of the most wonderful, beautiful, kindest man I've ever met. It's been a breathless whirlwind ever since. The *Wicked Darlings* final book is set to release into the world three weeks after we get off our honeymoon. Perfect for the new year.

Already, the presales have tripled from the last book, and personally, I think the finale is the best book of all. It's funny, gut-wrenching, and he wrapped up the loose ends with meticulous precision.

Pam already has the launch party planned.

Since he made his residence a permanent thing, Silver Creek pulled Chase in, and hasn't let him go. He's a town favorite, and not because he has a secret identity. He's the Mr. Rogers of friendly neighbors, and I love it about him. Always helping clean rain gutters, move furniture, fix tires. Anything, Chase is the guy on speed dial.

One of the best things is his connection with the Grahams.

They're my people, but now they're Chase's too. I think Sloan loves him as much as me since he's basically Rowan's bromance buddy, and gives the surly innkeeper a guy to veg with.

I smile as Sloan and Rowan dance on the wooden floor with baby Scarlet. The little girl has a tuft of dark hair and a frown that rivals her daddy's, but a smile like her mommy. Abigail and her tween brigade keep giggling as Noah Hayden and a few other actors from the show bounce and dance around their little fan club with the patience of older—extra famous —brothers and sisters.

Behind them, Chase's parents and sister chat with my mom, and Marcia and Tom Halverson, Heather's parents. Her entire family—including her sisters—flew out to support us.

I've met them several times. Whenever Chase flew out to Los Angeles to offer his consultations on the set, we would stop and see them. They're wonderful, and have accepted me as part of their family. To some it might be strange, but I'm grateful to the Halversons, and to Heather, for loving Chase. For showing him what *he* deserves in love.

Chase stands. His fitted tux shows off the strength of his body, and I can't keep my eyes off him. He tugs on the sleeves, then holds out his hand. "Dance with me, Wife."

"Husband, I thought you'd never ask." I bat my lashes and take his hand.

He pulls me close, and soon enough I forget we're not alone.

To think I almost resigned that I would never have this in my life. I can't imagine a day without Chase Thorn. He's become my life, my love, my best friend. He inspires me. Sometimes when we cook together, he'll toss out an idea, I'll run with it, and next thing I know it's on the menu at the Honey Pot.

The same goes for him. Already, he's brainstorming a new idea for a new fantasy world. My favorite nights are cuddled close, dreaming up faraway lands and wicked villains with each other.

Chase brushes his lips against my ear, drawing me back to this moment. "I love you, Jeri. I promise I always will."

I kiss him, sweet and slow. "I love you, Rex Blade, Chase Thorn, and whatever name you come up with when you start writing romance."

He snorts a laugh. "Don't hold your breath for that."

"I'm not going to let the idea die. The way you made my heart race with Kage and the Huntress, mmmm-yes."

He laughs and shakes his head, and I get my reward in the cute flush to his cheeks. I love embarrassing him about his books. He's so darn humble; I can't get enough. I kiss him again, then whisper against his lips. "No matter what, you have my heart."

"And that's all I need."

It's true. His heart is all I'll ever need.

Want More?

In all my eBooks I offer bonus scenes so readers can enjoy a little more with the book boyfriends and the ladies who love them. Scan the QR code below and you can enjoy a digital bonus scene with Jeri and Chase. If you have any trouble, feel free to email em@emilycauthor.com and we'll get you squared away.

Thank You

Thank you to all my readers for your endless support. I love writing these stories, and nothing makes me happier than knowing other people enjoy them too.

Thank you to my family for encouraging this journey, and thank you to Dad for your love of Hallmark Christmas--without your insistence I might never have written a Christmas romance at all. Thank you to Sara Sorensen for your job smoothing out the hard edges, catching the messes with my timeline and misspellings. Thank you to Blue Water Books for creating these holiday covers!

I am so grateful to you all!

Em

Made in the USA
Columbia, SC
19 October 2023

24692245R00114